Reincarnation
—or Madness?

A light flicked on, yellow light.

Her head swam for a moment, she felt limp, she was looking into the eyes of Milan, who held her by the wrists.

Her left hand hurt; it was still clutching the great metal medallion. She turned it, saw blood and hair, gasped and choked, dropped it, even as she saw that it was clean; there was no hair, no blood.

Milan looked stern and gloomy. Gently he lowered her hands. She slumped toward him, walking weakly to the staircase, and sat down on the steps.

"What skeleton did I uncover now?" she asked.

"You're the only one who saw it all," Milan said.

CAPE HOUSE

L. P. Shepherd

A DELL BOOK

TO R²

Published by
Dell Publishing Co., Inc.
1 Dag Hammarskjold Plaza
New York, New York 10017

Dell ® TM 681510, Dell Publishing Co., Inc.
Published in association with Seymour Lawrence, Inc.
Printed in the United States of America
First printing—January, 1974

SHE WALKED as though on stilts, hardly bent her knees. And sometimes tottered one step back, a lone figure with long tawny hair.

There were long, easy blasts from the Bay. But impersonal. That is, not to bless, not to kill. And cold.

The tension in Blanch's jaw, the frozen muscles. What seemed like tranquility on her lovely clear features was a sudden chill and rock hardness. *Not again. Not again.*

Theirs—hers. The new, though already weathered, shingled cottage. The Stowe Cottage. Aaron with blue lips, looking at books, making believe he was reading. Perhaps reading. So formally holding a volume for the past hours, open to the flyleaf. And Edna, always in her room, watching for birds, or looking over her long handwritten business notes; the renting of three of their cottages and whatever business with the Boston banks.

Great for Blanch. A great start.

She stopped and looked at the engagement ring.

From Tod. Gone, over the Tonkin Gulf.

Rumination didn't loosen her stilt-stiff knee-caps.

It wasn't the shock. That had happened months before. And had Tod ever really existed?

Or, for that matter, she?

He'd been a nice guy. A crew-cutted boy scout with some depths. She felt no sorrow.

Would it have been as cold as Aaron and Edna's marriage seemed to have been?

Something happened about twenty yards away, in one of the Spanish outbuildings, stucco despite its being right on Cape Cod Bay. Again.

One of the doors opened. Not fell open or was opened. She waited and looked into the black entrance, could see well into it.

No one emerged, or stood there.

Late afternoon, not yet twilight.

She stilted on to the main house.

It had been left to her by her mother, under the executorship of her grandparents, Aaron and Edna. Unable or not caring to maintain it, unable to sell it, they had given it to the Venturian order for a seminary, thus getting more, at the time, as a tax benefit, than they would have gotten on the market, or than it had ever been worth.

Within fifteen years acolyte admissions fell away from fifty-five young men to six. It became eerie, the long building with its graceful outbuildings, and only one light on in the early evening, and finally no light.

Then workmen who had no idea who was taking over or for what purpose, removed the eccle-siastical items and the cross from under the eaves of the main building, and the trio of sacred stat-ues from the shrine.

And on their heels, one light burned again. Only now there seemed to be only one occupant (more than the seminary had toward the end). Mr. Mallkin, a fat buoyant man with a thin nose very high up on his face, and jet black suits that, with his walk, made you wonder if you had just seen him in a cassock. He seemed to be alone ex-cept for the once-a-week groundsman, who had worked for the seminarians.

And every once in a while, weeks apart, per-haps a month, there would be a score of cars, many of them expensive, parked on the grounds, and lights.

But it was only at night and they drove off be-fore dawn.

Yellow orangey, the buildings. Blanch was nev-er one for color. Now it was more so, burning against the darkening Bay, blooded with the rose of the about-to-plunge sun.

She pressed the bell and felt that it wasn't ring-ing. She knocked, her fingers futile on the heavy paneled wood. She tried the door. It opened easi-ly and swiftly.

She winced at the desolation before her, the hard "woodiness" of the great hall and balcony above, the uncarpeted staircase; and the mass moving toward her.

Mr. Mallkin, with his buttocks and thighs thick

and tight against his silky ecclesiastical suit with its short jacket, floated, sailed to her like the cliché Spanish galleon with all its sails billowing.

"My dear girl," he said, as though in the middle of a speech, "I've been typing all week and I simply can't type all week—all day, for that matter. I must have someone to type. It will be three dollars an hour. You may select your own hours and come when you choose. I hope you are happy."

As he was talking, somehow he was guiding her, without touching or gesturing, walking just beside and behind her, though out of arms' reach, through the great hall, through what the seminarians had used as the dining hall or refectory, into what once had been the conservatory with its wall of bulging glass.

In it now were two tables made of unpainted doors lying on sawhorses and an immense board-of-directors table, the sides and legs heavy and ornate. All the tables were stacked with piles of papers, magazines, and seedy-backed books.

He led her to a fluted, hourglass of a bentwood chair with a velvet, tasseled cushion, before an office typewriter that was crowded onto the table.

Beside it were a mass of manuscript pages two feet high, and a few sheets of typescript. A partially typed sheet was in the machine.

He had not stopped talking and in their procession had said, savoring each word, getting more out of each than he should, "It has been so oppressive. Possibly the climate. What it has done to my moods! There's that awful throbbing, as though I were the Bay. And yet to look at it you wouldn't sense a throbbing at all. It has totally destroyed any tendency on my part to employ my skills. Will this do?"

Blanch sat, touched the keys, said, "Actually, the table is too high. But then the chair is high."

She turned to him.

There was neither repulsion nor liking in his eyes. In fact, it was he who seemed to be struggling for acceptance. Yet his was not a face, it was too ludicrous with the high nose, the expanse above his upper lip, his owl eyes even more owled by the black frames of his glasses.

"I shall have a typewriter table and appropriate chair for you tomorrow."

"I can do some typing today."

"I am glad."

Had the outer door opened since she'd come in? They must have left it open.

She glanced at the great north window behind her. The pane frames seemed to converge, bulge in and out like a lung.

"I shall leave the manse door open for you always. I am occupied. Farewell until tomorrow. And if you do not see me when you come, pray don't consider it a slight."

"How many copies? Do you want copies?"

He startled, shuffled, began to bray a "Hem hem hem," said, "One can't carbon hundreds, perhaps thousands."

"Just for your records."

"Hundreds from one good copy perhaps," he rambled. Was he serious?

"It can be Xeroxed."

"Hem hem hem—yes, that's it. Xerox. Xerox Clorox Hydrox. Ha!" His little joke. "And now I shall leave you."

Blanch waited.

He turned and floated—no, soared?—out.

The door was closed. He had shut the door.

She went to the great window.

Mad—the Lockes; then Aaron and Edna, Quakers; then the Roman Catholics; then Mr. Mallkin. She thought she could see Aaron and Edna's place, through the writhy pines, suspected she couldn't. Yet they lived close-by.

She wondered what these modest Quakers had thought of the house she was standing in, how they felt when they had lived in it with her. But one never talked to Aaron and Edna about such things.

"I am the ghost of Hamlet's father."

"Swear!"

"Swear!"

"Swear!"

"Three times did they swear!"

The handwriting on the manuscript pages was immense, juvenile. Yet flawlessly clear.

be well covered, and there is as little radiating surface as possible, the above assumption that there is no loss of heat in passing through may be nearly, though never quite, correct. On the other hand it is more than likely to be very far from correct, and, to eliminate any errors of this kind, one might recommend a so-called calibration. This, again, involves an assumption which is open to some doubt, which is that when in a quiescent state, it will drop

In the sheet on the typewriter:

these, experiments were made on four passages across the tubes. A drum at right angle to the line of tubes was tried, but as no provision was made for securing dryness the results were

The typing was execrable. She would have to do over the sheets already typed. She sought paper, in doing so, surveyed the junk on the tables. *Love Stories.* "*Thirty Real Life Tales for 5¢.*" 1936. A pile of other ancient popular magazines beneath and beside it. A book *Sunlight in a Dark World.* No author, mildewed red binding. Three volumes of *The Book of Knowledge.* And manuscripts, piles of them on aged paper.

At last, a fresh ream of paper in a box. Good.

She began to type. This would be difficult, the purpose so unclear. As in her high-school typing course, and now for the second time, she would have to train herself to see the copy without reading it; to type words, or whatever it is that went to the fingers.

It worked. She felt herself in sort of a cloudy soup, oblivion, the words appearing on paper, words and punctuation. She dared, briefly, to think of other things, then checked her typing. It could be done. She would think of other things.

But the height of the typewriter was absurd now, painful. She would only work for an hour.

It seemed interminable. Would she last an hour? She glanced at her watch. She had been typing for an hour and seventeen minutes. She would type on, but must train herself to take ten-minute breaks every hour.

> within seven and one-half per cent of the highest theoretical

Would she die in Shoreham? As eventually, though they'd held it off phenomenally, Aaron and Edna would? Blanch had left her job in preparation for Tod's demobilization. She had been in a publishing office in Manhattan, not particularly caring for the job, although for a bit she enjoyed being a professional and a real New Yorker. And then he'd been lost. The shock had not been as traumatic as one would think. And Blanch had appreciated her grandparents' lack of response to the whole matter—they'd lived too long. But then she'd contracted what they first thought was mononucleosis and then discovered it to be a brain tumor.

She had come through the one or both very well—after almost seven months. Not even a bad scar under her hair. But then something possibly worse followed, her staying on the Cape this fall. The sudden stop to her life from the progression of live-in prep school, school in Switzerland, scholarship years at Jackson, her job. It was not so much a fear of going out in the world again, as an inability, momentary, she hoped, to start up again. And that awful, common danger when one returns to one's home, the sudden feeling of infantilism, of being inferior to one's elders and the world.

She had thought this typing job might become some sort of a start, a renewal of her life and work, such as they were.

required varies with the kind and condition of the fuel, and thickness in the

This was absurd, it was dark already, almost dark, at least dark inside. The great window was a wall that was lighter, but did not let in light. She was almost reading in the dark.

Two and a half hours. Why not?

She could work half and quarter hours as well.

Perhaps that was her trouble—her always wanting to finish things on the zero—

The door was open.

She was sure that she had seen Mr. Mallkin shut it.

She went to it, over the naked wooden floor, almost closed the door, then tapped it slightly. It didn't budge. Then she shut the door. Plenty of sound. She opened it again. A distinct sound from the latch. Though she might have overlooked it while typing.

She hurried to the front door, looking with distaste at the uncarpeted staircase, trying not to look at the balcony it reached.

Outside, the shadows were nervous. A loud crowd of birds passed.

No point in cutting across, although she might try it some time. Meanwhile she would have to leave by the ornamental arch onto the highway. Was it the entrance or exit for the seminary?

Perfunctorily she glanced at the outbuilding, was sure she saw the door close. So much of that lately. Not hallucination, she felt certain. Nor important, for that matter.

MILAN SAT or rather crouched in the living room, since he was six feet seven and almost every known chair was an indignity to him. He had been reading the *Christian Century* with as great an intensity as he would a *J. C. Whitney Car Parts and Accessories Catalog*. Now he stood, stooping against the threat of the ceiling.

Blanch didn't smile, nor reject Milan, in his sweatshirt and jeans and moccasins. This was only the third time she'd encountered him. Although she found something comforting in his long, unsmiling face.

Edna came (Had she retreated to her room?) said, "We didn't wait dinner for you."

"Good that you didn't. I just forgot time."

"Well look, I haven't eaten yet," Milan said. "Maybe we could get a bite in Orleans."

"That will be nice," Blanch said.

Edna seemed to be thinking this over with great seriousness, said, "You've got the key," as she started for her room. And then, "Good evening, Mr. Hoxha."

"Good evening, Mrs. Stowe," he said with equal seriousness.

Darn! The houseside door of Milan's car had just swung open.

He glanced at it and Blanch, then said, "I hadn't really shut it."

Blanch laughed. "You've noticed."

He had an odd smile on the small mouth in his long face.

"Well, each time, a door either opened or shut," he recalled.

"So you did notice that." Blanch laughed, relieved.

They ate fried clams with French fries on cardboard dishes, with coffee in plastic containers. The last time it had been a foreign movie, with Milan noncommittal.

"Would you care to see my work?"

This wasn't really sudden. Blanch nodded.

He was living in a barnlike camp cottage on the Bay, a few miles from the Stowes. He had aquaria, a microscope, a projector microscope, a screen, and artist materials. Otherwise the place was bare, except for the furniture that rented with the house for the summer crowds.

"It's going to be cold this winter," Blanch said, looking at the uninsulated walls.

"I know. This is my third winter here."

"What do you do in the summers?"

"I work in Florida. I mean, for money."

The paintings were large and, Blanch felt, superb—of some sort of microscopic life, in the bravest of colors, both subjects and backgrounds, yet not garish but subtly related. Though possibly not saleable. She couldn't picture people hanging them in their homes for aesthetic reasons. And somehow they seemed too lyrical if the taste of what was manifest in, say, the Museum of Natural History in Manhattan, set the standard. But this was his thing, and more power to him.

"I'm awed," Blanch said. "I don't know what to think yet. They're so unusual, so— What is your name?"

"It's Albanian. But we're really Yugoslavs."

"I was going to say," she laughed, "now that you've told me—Yugoslavian. But I don't know how they paint."

"It could be. I'm first generation. My father came here to escape the police."

"Political?" Blanch understood.

"As a matter of fact, I think he was legitimately criminal."

Was he kidding?

"What a thing to confess to."

"I don't think I inherited that tendency."

He brought out the end of a half-gallon of red wine, poured two small cheese glasses.

"Your grandmother told me you're working."

"Yes. As a start."

"There seems to be something unusual about the place."

"Yes? Why do you say that?"

He lit the fire, then said, "I jog. It depends on the tide. This may sound crazy, but it was after midnight a couple of weeks ago. All the lights on the Bay side were on and there seemed to be a lot of people inside. It was balmy and the wind was coming offshore and there seemed to be all sorts of movement. But there was complete silence. It may have just been atmospheric. But it was eerie."

"Did you investigate?"

He smiled, his little smile. "I wasn't concerned then."

"And now you're concerned."

Blanch relented. Yet the Cape winter crowd were a nosey lot, the permanents, and she certainly wasn't going to start any stories.

"He's having me type an endless scientific thing," she said.

Milan's eyes flattened at her tight reply. He must have been extending help if and when she needed it; he had not withdrawn it, and that was that.

Help for what?

She rather liked him. That is, compared with Tod. Tod would never have run at night. Or served the end, rather vinegary, of a bottle of wine. Tod was always all cooperation. This giant —what was it, Yugo or Czecho-slav?—seemed all give.

She was amused, after her dates in Manhattan, that there was never an approach—verbal, physical, ocular—from him. She wondered if Milan might not have learned this from—had he said his father was a swindler? Why didn't she remember these things?

He told her about the things he painted, about the creature that looked like a thinly decorated Christmas tree and was so tiny it lived in the moisture between two grains of shore sand.

At last she said, "This has been fun. I want to go now."

He helped her into her car coat and drove her home.

"We'll do this again," he suggested at the door.

"Next time I'll buy," Blanch said.

"We'll discuss it then." That long, quiet, friendly face.

From her dormer window she glanced at the big house. She could see it and the front door, over the evergreens. And as she looked, there was no door, but a black slot, and a flashlight shone out straight. And nothing more. It kept burning, staring out. At least it was small enough to be a flashlight beam, the type of light with a translucent red plastic collar.

No one emerged, no one entered.

When she looked again there was only the door, shut.

EACH ATE separately. Blanch wondered if Aaron ate at all. He would toy with a cold piece of stewed meat. She would see it in a sauce dish for days, in and out of the refrigerator, it seemed, always before him when he sat at the kitchen table. Edna's portions were harsh and birdlike, harsh in that they may have been an explorer's emergency rations. Blanch's breakfasts and lunches were nothing to speak of, but for supper she would eat steak and soup, the latter canned. It was almost as though she were back in Manhattan. And of course salads.

This morning as she came down, Edna was finishing her tea, and a sauce dish of cornflakes.

"Mr. Mallkin telephoned," she said, "to tell you that the previous time arrangement continued. But that today you were not to come before one and not to stay after four."

"I suppose I ought to bring an alarm clock. I lost track of time yesterday."

"He also suggested that you leave a statement of your time expenditure beside the typewriter when you leave."

"Good."

Edna's serious eyes behind the thick lenses.

Not distorting, like the type of lenses with concentric rings in them like the bottom of a bottle, but eye-enlarging and thick. Blanch wished that Edna would ask her about the job. About Milan. About anything.

But it had always been that way, even when she was a girl. Bubbling over with something to say, for a while she would say it. Edna would listen intently, with troubled eyes. As though whatever had been said was profoundly ponderable, possibly contestable. But too much the lady and Quaker, she would not contest it, would look at it fairly, and try to conceal her doubts.

As for Aaron, there had never been any contact. Perhaps he had been articulate in his office. Although Blanch didn't believe that as a bank lawyer he'd had to appear in court. But he would return silently, from his short hours, look at Edna with the same sort of look she had for Blanch's confidences, and then hold in his hands, presumably read, a book.

Yet Blanch felt that things weren't too bad. It had always been as though she were living in a quiet hotel.

She had coffee and orange juice, and wondered if she should plan getting back to Manhattan, write to some contacts. Or read. Or, she mused, like the Chinese soothsayer, "decide that it was a good day to take a journey or a bath." But she had already showered, decided to—

From the west window, in the kitchen, she could see Milan's lanky figure strolling out on the Bay. The tide was low, leaving an immense sweep of glistening sand. He was like a surrealist figure on a surrealist plane.

This was pushing it. But it seemed to be a to-heck-with-everything morning.

She changed to jeans and a bulky sweater, and canvas oxfords, tripped down the back steps, strolled to the beach, and out onto the dewatered Bay, bypassing puddles with their thin traffic of hermit crabs.

Milan started toward her but she waved him to stay where he was. After an almost interminable walk (Why do empty vistas seem so much longer?) she reached him.

"Time out?" Blanch asked.

"I have to paint when it's dark. Because I have to project images of my models."

They strolled for a bit, gradually separating by dozens of yards, each busy with his own viewing.

At one point Milan took a small bottle from his pocket and bottled something.

The big house had shrunk in the distance to a trivial, brittle, gaudy little thing.

North, in the evergreens, Blanch could see Milan's rambling bungalow. Aaron and Edna's was hidden by trees. From their cottage you could see the Bay, but from the Bay you couldn't see the cottage.

The great flat waste about them was getting wetter. The tide, though imperceptible, was dangerously speeding back. They hurried to the beach.

"Have you always been here?" Milan asked.

"Heavens no. School, college—I lived and worked in Manhattan for a year."

"Do you like it here?"

"I could," Blanch said.

She stopped, looked up at him, smiled.

"Do you like it here?"

His small, quizzical smile. And dark, warm eyes.

"Here. Florida. I suppose anywhere near water."

"Even a mud puddle."

"It would have what I want, too."

Blanch found it unusual to be so interested in forms of life that weren't people.

"I'd like to take you to Woods Hole one day," he said, "and show you what they're doing in oceanography."

There may have been a cloud on Blanch's face. The thought that she didn't care about oceanography—about anything, disturbed her.

He sensed something, dropped it, said, "What's it like in that big house? When I'm walking past it, especially on the beach, it seems so intact and solid, with nothing inside."

"It's—just empty," she said.

He suppressed further questions, walked her to the kitchen steps.

"It must be your lunchtime. Let me make you a sandwich."

It was Edna who discouraged him from wanting to come in. Or Edna and Aaron, if Milan had seen Blanch's grandfather. She couldn't blame Milan. The cottage was like a morgue, in a way, to a stranger. To a stranger?

"I'll see you," Milan said. A hopeful question. His eyes lively.

"Of course," Blanch said.

That was that. She was walking more easily today. And there was sun on the evergreens and leafy trees and grass.

She ran up to her bedroom and gasped. Looked with amazement, a confused smile that was no smile.

Like a malign starfish, a great flat black crystal star, over a foot across, lay on the coverlet of her bed.

She looked at it, strangely hesitant about approaching or touching it. At last she sat on the bed, kept studying it. Somehow it made her think of a crab. Jet black and catching light. She touched it. It was cold. Sharp edged and reassuringly hard. It seemed to have been cut from a single crystal. What would the material have been? Onyx? Blanch didn't know stones. Geological or lapidary. The star was not heavy but had weight. Somehow it fascinated her like a reverse crystal. The type in which one saw lovely visual distortions that seemed to draw you in. But this seemed to bounce you out against darkness. There was nothing in it indicating its decorative use—no hole for a pendant (What a size!) nor hook to hang it on the wall. Weird.

Not really deciding, Blanch placed it in the top drawer of her bureau, on top of slips. It was huge, took up much of the drawer. And then she shut it, ran down, wanted to run into Edna's room and ask, and did not. Dared not.

She prepared a lunch snack in the kitchen.

Edna came in.

"The star?" Blanch was gay.

Edna seemed worried, concerned. Always.

"You're almost twenty-four," she said. "Your mother once spoke of your having it. I was sorting things and came across it. I had been meaning to."

"Well, is there a—? I mean, how did my mother use it?"

"I don't know. She showed it to me after one of their trips. She made much of it, I don't recall why, and especially suggested that you would have it. Though I don't believe she ascribed any pecuniary value to it."

Blanch was a bit amused, a bit angry. "You just forgot about it."

Edna's expression was the same. But then, Blanch had always felt that if she had done something really mad, cut off a finger in front of them, or set fire to the rug, Aaron and Edna would just have looked, in the way Edna looked at her now. How could you beat something like that? That look of some disapproval, some concern. Maybe it was only naïve shyness. But it was infuriating.

"I had been meaning to. But it escaped me."

Perhaps if Edna had really cared, made a big to-do about it for a birthday. But then, Quakers didn't. Or at least the Stowes.

"Thanks awfully," Blanch said. "Although I don't know what I can do with it."

"It is yours to do with what you will," Edna said.

SHE ARRIVED at two. The door was unlocked. She didn't take the trouble to knock. The great hall was the same, in fact its impact diminished by familiarity. *"One could adjust to purgatory."* Had that been said? The refectory was bright and empty. Even the conservatory was brighter.

Despite its north wall of glass, it was a dark room. The windows toward the road, and opposite them, to the Bay, were long narrow slits. Not small, really, but small in proportion to the dimensions of the room and height of the ceiling. Which made for cool shadows despite the brightness of the day.

Immediately, Blanch could see that her typescript had been removed. She was glad that she had marked the manuscript page where she had stopped, and indicated the number of the next typed page.

It was almost with affection that she attacked the manuscript.

that the evaporation should equal at least 9 pounds of water from a temperature of 180°

It was all so superbly meaningless to her, the words that she was typing. With occasional glances at the Bay, with its great metal wreck of a target ship like a painted ship upon a painted sea, and glances at the grounds on the other side of the house, and the highway beyond—

The door swung open (It shouldn't have opened silently now.) to Mr. Mallkin.

Blanch felt silly. She hadn't noticed the metal typewriter table the machine now stood on, nor the swivel chair she'd been sitting on, the pieces used but good.

"Are the appurtenances satisfactory? Oh my, the complications of one trying to live the simplest of lives. The telephone calls alone, you know. And then you must have receipts for everything. You must have receipts."

Even as he went on, with words Blanch no longer heard, she felt a sluggishness, a slowing of her heart, something that had recurred since the operation. As though her heart and innards were being dragged down. She looked hard to see Mr. Mallkin, finally did, his bloated white not-too-clean shirt and unpressed black tie, his sharp wedge of a jaw and small mouth, high small wedge of a nose, great owl eyes.

She found herself saying, "There will have to be spare ribbons, type cleaner, erasers. A copy stand will help."

And he, almost as though he were part of her malaise, or affected by it, said, "Would you arrange for those at Nicholl's Stationery and Books and charge them to me. It was they who procured the table and chair," his eyes never pertinent to the words but tentative, as though watching, as though hiding behind their sockets, the words or her apprehension of them slow, sluggish.

And then he wasn't there. The room was empty, the door shut. Her heart was beating strongly, almost as though in a seizure. It accelerated even more when she discovered she was five pages beyond where she thought she would be.

Well, that was something.

She glanced down at her watch and shuddered. There were thin symmetrical scratches on her wrist just above the back of her hand, each bar about three-quarters of an inch long. Thinner than hair, but the skin was broken, the tiny cross was of blood, yet too shallow to be oozing or running. Merely a red cross of her blood.

She gasped nervously and rushed to the door, it was open, through the refectory, to the washroom that she knew was behind the great staircase.

It was the same as it had been but for the row of pharmacist brown half-gallon bottles, each with a rubber stopper, each with code letters and numbers on adhesive tape labels; and on the toilet tank cover, a glass bowl of thin glass pipes.

She washed her hands, especially the scar, so thin that she could almost rub it away with her thumb, avoided the dingy towel by drying her hands with her own Kleenex.

The afternoon was souring. The door was open to the front lawn, it hadn't been a moment before. From bright and gold and blue the light had now taken on a yellow tinge, like an aged bandage. Reluctantly she returned, through the refectory. The door to the refectory was closed now. She had left it open.

When, as a tot, she had lived for a short time with Edna and Aaron in this house, they had all sorts of plants against the north window. But before—she was sure that it had been a grand room, with a concert piano and Turkish carpets and tasseled hangings, with perhaps (No, she knew!) a great potted fronded plant before the window. And there had been—there had been—yes, shields and weapons and armor over the Bay windows. And a tapestry—and some paintings hung absurdly high—over the opposing windows. And there had been the great green vase—malachite? —it was French and—

Blanch shuddered. Absurd. All she had ever seen, it's a wonder she remembered, was the great areas of space, of emptiness and bleak Morris chairs and wicker tables, that's all that had ever been there in her lifetime. Probably a dream. But she hadn't dreamed. Or an illustration in a book or magazine.

Yet she— She went to the door, looked hard at the floor. Kneeled, felt, was sure she felt, though so slight, the circular indentation made by the base of the vase.

And felt a strange quiet comfort.

But not coming over her. Rather a strange dispersal or dispersion of self. A non-response, plus someone else's response.

She arose with difficulty, found her knees stiff, the old stilt walk, yet she hardly acknowledged this as she returned to the typewriter, typed another eleven pages, warmly and distantly, unable to dispel the feeling or vision of the tapestries, a long medieval hunt tapestry of unusual shape, and another of a musical party, the women in wimples and pointed hats and the men in hats that looked like inverted flower pots.

It was dark. Again she had forgotten to put on the light, which would have come from the chandeliers high above. She left her time slip on top of the typed pages, weighted the stack with a heavy medallion she discovered on the board-of-directors table, let herself out.

She had difficulty climbing the steps to her house. Not difficulty really, but she had to yank at the railing. Rather, found it convenient to do so.

She entered by the front door.

Edna's hand was raised almost to her chin. Aaron sat with an open book. Yes, to the back flyleaf. He always sat that way, and couldn't be taken seriously. But in Edna's eyes there was more than Blanch was used to finding.

"Is there anything wrong?" Blanch's words dragged.

Edna nodded "No," falsely it seemed, for the nod had begun with a question, which continued.

"I'll eat later," Blanch said, struggled up to her room, sat in her small upholstered armchair before a dormer window looking toward the Bay.

It was quite dark now but the Bay retained
light, revealing the still low tide, the great vast
vista level, with shallow bars and hollows. Should
she, Blanch wondered, worry about herself?
What was there to worry about? She was, she
lived. She couldn't see ahead, true—yet didn't
miss it. The long hospital stay and recuperation
had taught her sloth, no vice despite all the current and past attacks on it.

Perhaps this was what the Orientals called con-
templation. Or a condition beyond even that.

But what if it were not, instead was a psycho-
pathological loss of identity?

She chilled, although her consciousness still
could not take the threat seriously. But, a rational
person, she decided to see her physician. She
phoned and was told to run right over, to see him
before his office hours began.

She announced the borrowing of the Dart,
drove the three miles to Dr. Wemyss. He was a
solid, large-mouthed, Roman-profiled wedge in
his seventies. The office furniture and medical
equipment predated him.

The moment she entered his office, his eyes
flashed, his mouth seemed to shape a silent "So!"
His usual smile was absent. He hadn't been her
physician for the operation.

"Sit down."

He tapped her knees with a rubber hammer.
He asked her to raise her arms, while he worked,
and had her do other stretches.

Meanwhile saying, "Doctors frequently do this

sort of thing in silence, Blanch. They may be preoccupied with what they're doing, or sadistically letting the patient sweat. Your responses are all adequate but slow, which can be attributed to the weather, your psychic attitude of the moment, fatigue, laziness. You're all right and it's not organic. Was there anything else you wanted to see me about?"

"I don't know."

He wrapped her arm for the blood pressure test.

"Silly," she said, "I felt as though something were pulling me down inside. *Were* inside. But it was so trivial I was embarrassed to call. And because I was embarrassed and felt it was trivial, I felt that I had better call."

"Good thinking. Let us decide that it's nothing."

"What was my mother like?"

He froze.

He removed the bandage, sat back, that unfamiliar hardness in his face.

"Edna would never tell you, would she?" A mere comment.

"No."

"She was very much like you. Now."

Then, "She wasn't ill?"

"No. It was the accident. The disaster."

Blanch wasn't listening to the last. The words came. *And why did you say "now"?*

"Then there's nothing?"

"No." He started to write a prescription,

bunched the pad sheet in his fist. "I could write you a placebo. That's all it would be. I almost wish I could say something negative, to justify your fears." Yet even as he spoke he was looking at her with this hardness she was not used to from him.

Why couldn't she have it out with him? With Edna? With anybody? Whatever it was "to have out."

She stilt-walked to the door, turned.

The hard look. She turned and left, drove to Milan's cabin. The roads were black, the branches of the trees fluttery and nervous.

He was at his door before she reached it.

Between the car and the cabin her knees, her elbows seemed to soften, her mind not so much clearing as becoming easy, hers.

"I interrupted your work."

"I was taking a break. I'd like to take a break for a month."

"You're not getting to dislike your work?"

"No. But my back and shoulders are hurting like the dickens."

She looked at how low he had set his easel, said, "I shouldn't wonder."

"Once I had everything right," he said. "And I couldn't paint." Then—"Are you taking me up on dinner?"

She laughed. "You haven't eaten."

He glanced toward the kitchen. "I guess not. There are no dishes in the sink."

"I haven't either!"

"Then it's on me."

"No. It's just that I suddenly realized I hadn't eaten. And I decided to take you."

Milan considered this, decided against arguing with her, said, "That's okay by me."

As they approached the big house, driving south toward Brewster, suddenly Blanch felt drained again, dragged down within, her brain dulled or numbed, but just as suddenly, several miles later, her energy returned.

Obviously psychic, she decided.

THEY ATE AT a lobster-and-steak-house, not quite a restaurant and a little better than a stand. They had tepid roast beef sandwiches, salad, and coffee that was cold.

"You never talk about your parents," Milan said. "I told you about my father."

"I don't," Blanch said. Then, in case he thought her fresh, "I don't know about them. I mean, I know a few things, dimly remembered. But I was so young when they died. I don't know if they're memories or fantasies."

"Didn't your grandparents ever tell you?"

Blanch chuckled. "Aaron doesn't speak, period. Never did. Edna's what they call diffident."

"Are you sure it's only her?" Milan chided.

Blanch shrugged.

"Don't tell me you've never been curious."

"No. Perhaps I'm a coward. But I just can't say: 'Edna, your story or your life!' And after all, my father was their only child. I guess the ground rules are, you don't talk about him. And when you eliminate questions about him, there goes my mother, too."

Milan embarrassedly changed the subject.

They stopped on the main street of Orleans, the one running from ocean to Bay. There was nowhere really to walk—past the drug store, the closed candy shop and coffee house. They sat in Milan's old Mustang and just looked. In the direction of the Bay.

"Dover Beach," Blanch thought.

"I called at your place last night."

"I was walking on the beach," Milan explained.

"You are a late walker."

"I get worked up, working. Then I have to walk it off."

"How is it late at night?"

"I don't know. Sometimes it's a feeling of getting crowded. Strangled. That the Cape is a tiny hook and the East Coast is a little bulge and the oceans are just puddles."

"Strangled by what?"

He shrugged.

"That's gloomy."

"I don't get that too much. But that's what I wanted to see you about tonight."

Blanch waited.

"I saw three men coming out of the big house.

I mean just shadows. They went a ways and then they saw me. They stopped, I kept walking. Then they seemed to hesitate, and then they went back to the house."

"Hm. Guests."

"Then I came across five—I suppose you'd call them altar candles—stuck in the sand. They were in the shape of a cross. The wicks were black."

"Isn't that strange? What do you make of it?"

"I don't know what to make of it." He laughed. "Maybe they're signaling for an angel to land." Then, somberly, "I worry about you all alone in that big house."

"If you don't know it, it does sound a bit scary. But since it's almost totally unfurnished, the atmosphere is really innocent."

"Then where does Mallkin live?"

"Oh I've never been on the upper floors." It was a pleasant feeling, having someone concerned. Perhaps she should be more concerned about herself. What was she doing on the Cape? Should she go back to Manhattan? Even to San Francisco? It was easy, just sort of goofing on from day to day.

A NEUTRAL day. Neither ecstatically sunfilled nor gloomy. As she approached the big house, a window in the attic swung shut.

Great! Blanch decided.

Used to not knocking, she opened the main door, stepped in. Mallkin was standing beside the stairs talking to a stranger, a tall young man. They turned to Blanch.

Blanch paused, nodded, hurried toward the refectory, taking with her the young man's smile. He had been dressed in an expensive sweater, with yachting ducks and shoes.

She sat at her typing stand, inserted paper, suddenly stopped, arose, walked back to the board-of-directors table she had just passed. How could she have missed it? A cat-o'-nine-tails. Rather small, with a long handle. Somehow it seemed inoffensive. She lifted one of the pellets at the end of a flail. It was not lead. More like a glob of thickened sap or resin. That was a consolation, she supposed.

And then she noted that the directors table had been partially cleared—perhaps eight feet of it. She found herself looking closer with inspired sleuthing.

There were no indications of manacles, straps or chains.

How lurid can one get?

Perhaps this was the time for her to pull out of this mad job and place. Yet she suddenly felt two emotions strange to her. One, the policeman or asylum attendant in us all, the irrational toughness that comes in us as a feeling that we can handle the socially maimed, and a bit of a thrill at the game. And the other, the down-drawing of the night before, the feeling that it would be hard to break any habit, even so short-lived a one as this job.

With that dullness returning to her mind, she set to typing, finally refused the bottle, the spoon, the glass on the tray, dismissed the maid with her eyes, turned them to the peacock feathers in the great malachite vase.

"No, Paxton," she said. "We can easily accommodate twenty for din—"

And then found she'd typed many pages, and that she was ravenously hungry.

It was almost two. This was absurd. She left the papers as they were, almost ran from the house, a bit wobbly with hunger, more disturbed, in her weakness, it seemed, by the outbuilding doors not opening or closing as she passed them.

At home the Dart was gone. She let herself in, ate two fruit yogurts as the soup heated, and with that a thick cheese sandwich.

Bloated, she leisured back to the big house. It was the emptiest and stillest of places, the windows shut as though they'd never been opened. One in the second-floor north room was slightly ajar, as if that screened place alone were a black mesh for Pandora's Box, a gangrenous wound. Who had built such large houses and why? They were crowding the tea table, with their fragile parasols and great straw hats, some waving to her.

Especially long, elegant—with his great stiff collar and cravat—interposing himself between Amanda and her—waving, he seemed especially effusive. Blanch hurried to them, as seemly as she could in her immense dress, the train of course pinned up, the spots in her veil sharpening yet softening the elegant scene, crowd, before her—

Broken field running on the grass.

What the devil would people think?

She stopped, turned again to the house. Was that someone at the conservatory window?

Her knees—stilt-walk. This was absurd. She rushed, forcing her knees to bend.

She seemed in full control now so long as she felt pugnacious, "assumed the virtue." She strode in. It was just past three, by her watch. The cross on her wrist wasn't there. She looked close. Perhaps the thinnest, whitest lines. In the conservatory the cleared part of the directors table was no longer cleared. *If it ever had been,* she decided ruefully.

She finished the half page she had left in the typewriter, whipped it out, inserted a fresh sheet.

Only it wasn't fresh. She stared at it, frozen. In the middle was typed

help*
help helphelphelp helpme helpm!

She looked about the room, at the windows, saw no one. Again she studied the plea. Could she have typed it? Was she trying to call to—herself? She didn't think so. Of this she was conditionally convinced by the quality of her previous typing. She had never committed such errors.

That was great. That was simply great! And

then she experienced what she could only describe as the feeling or sound of cardboard scraping against her teeth, or her teeth trying to rend thick cardboard.

How could she not have noticed, on the left of the door as she had come in, that large dark wardrobe or chifferobe?

It stood perhaps seven feet high, a foot off the floor, and was at least four feet across, perhaps as many deep.

What a hideous piece with its mausoleumlike domed top.

After all, Mallkin had every right to put any piece of furniture anywhere he wished.

She would not look into it.

She had no business looking into it.

She would lie in bed looking at it, it seemed for hours, for all night. Not really, because then the unbelievable would happen, nothingness—which was sleep—would come upon her. And then next morning the tremendous excitement of Cape sun, it was never dark for this child (only later), and in daylight the wardrobe would shrink considerably. Not that she liked it in the daylight either, although if she had to stay in the room during the day, she would leave the doors open. The secret door to the Bad Man's place could be in the back of course. And anyway it wasn't the same wardrobe. At night she felt that she had to watch or the door would open and the awful would emerge. But not so long as she kept her eyes open and watched it.

Her eyes widened to the sudden dead light, the beginning of a thin twilight. Twenty pages! Good or bad? She didn't know, she had never timed her typing, didn't recall what was good.

> some of the stayed surfaces were omitted and hand holes were substituted for the large

Enough of that! The wardrobe huddled against the wall, next to the door, like a neglected courtier. And fooey on you! But it was there and she hadn't looked at it, and that was that.

She was almost at the main door when the silence was rent by the most animallike shriek she had ever heard, a ringing inhuman agony made into sound. Chill played on her neck nape, her calves, her forearms. There was a running above, a panting, the shriek repeated, humanizing into the screaming plea, "Don't do it! God! Don't do— God!" a scuffle, a door slam on silence.

The ormolu table, the great china umbrella vases, the elegant gas chandelier turned down. She bunched her furs tighter about her, disregarded the footman as she stepped out, said a bitter "Bother!" for the strap that had broken on her Italian slipper.

She removed one sandal, walked a bit, felt silly and removed the other, though the ground was cool, and then she ran, this time cutting across the lawn between the outbuildings, to the brick wall that abutted the road beyond which was Aaron and Edna's house.

To get over the seven foot wall. Fun, she climbed a small sturdy pear tree, paused atop the wall.

There was a light in one of the attic windows of the big house. A black blob of head appeared and withdrew. She lowered herself on the tree again, so that she would not be silhouetted above the wall. Still the light. But nothing at the window.

She scrambled atop the wall. How was she going to get off it? Why should seven feet be so high? Throwing her sandals on the ground, she let herself down on the other side by scuffing her knees and feet and hands, with finally the awful last drop, so much a jolt because it was blind.

What an idiot!

Why hadn't she gone by the Bay side?

This had been some day!

THE NEXT day, as she appeared for work, an outbuilding door opened, something Blanch had gotten used to, but now the man with the delicate features stood in the doorway. With his radiant yet shy smile. And psychic wall. It was a general love, and he was not to be approached any further. Mr. Got-Rocks of the yachting uniform. Why did she feel that he was the one who had shrieked yesterday? Blanch smiled perfunctorily and went on.

Mr. Mallkin, letting himself out of the conservatory, looked worried.

"Did you see the young gentleman with whom I was speaking yesterday?"

"He was in the doorway of the north outbuilding."

"You're very perceptive," Mr. Mallkin sighed as he hurried to the door, his great hams in their tight trousers chugging as he hurried through the refectory.

> inspection of this table it will be seen why it is more viable to dry at the higher temperatures. The atmosphere is seldom saturated with the

She had done a good bunch of pages. Hardly— No! *Not* thinking of—not even noting—the content. She was mildly distressed, though, to realize that she had been not even thinking. Perhaps a sun-filled blah of a condition. With dots or blobs of people moving about inside and out.

The doors to both the refectory and the great hall were open. A truck had pulled up. There was scuffling and grunting and uttering of commands, and heavy feet clambering up the uncarpeted grand staircase.

It wasn't polite to evince interest. But of course mummy and Paxton had everything under control. It would be the radiators attached to the new furnace. No cold rooms anymore, no fireplace to be warned to keep away from.

There was a scuffle on the stairs. Blanch went

to the refectory door and looked out. Two workers were struggling with a huge bench covered in leather, with some chrome fixtures. Mallkin was fluttering nervously above. A small, broad-shouldered old man stood lower on the steps.

"You bend at the knees damnit," he was saying. "And watch out for the banister. I'll not have it battered anymore than it is."

"We could have done just as well with blankets on a table," Mallkin said.

"We could have done just as well with my foot in your backside, Sir!"

"There is no need for vulgarity. You've given me trouble enough."

The little man had a long head with black hair up to his bald dome, which he rubbed nervously with immense hands. It was the head of one of those hermits one sees in Chinese or Japanese prints.

Place is getting crowded, Blanch decided.

Thirsty, she went to where she recollected the kitchen being. It seemed larger than she recalled, the sort of place banquets could be prepared in, with great steel coffee urns, and vats, and a center aisle of work tables and shelves. It was fantastic, there was simply nothing there, no pots, no plates except, thank heavens, an empty jam jar above one of the sinks. Somehow it seemed to make all the difference. In what, she wasn't sure. She dared to go to the refrigerator, a whole room with a hideous varnished wooden wall. Now it was empty and unchilled. The door still looked sinister, with its large hinges and latch, although Blanch was sure, pretty sure, that you could let yourself out from within. And in the kitchen there was a large metal refrigerator, also turned off, that made her shudder and think of mortuaries.

Where did Mallkin eat? And the others. Unless one of the outbuildings was a porter's lodge.

The staff's Olympian welcomes the (one?) time she ran in, her blond hair flying, her white dress with its white ribbon belt, and white stockings and white high-button shoes. And the frilly things the maids wore on their heads, and Paxton, with his immense jaw and sideburns, and walleye that was so terrifying yet somehow so appropriate for the head butler.

She screamed, caught herself almost at the beginning, almost ran to the conservatory. What would they say to her screaming in kitchens? She shuddered, remembering Paxton coming upon her once as she explored the servants' floor, under the roof. Silently he spun her around, his great face hanging over hers, then pulled at the hair beside her ears, out and hard. Oh how it had hurt, diabolically painful.

He said, "This you shall never report, or it will go the worse for you."

Was Paxton a sadist? Now that she thought of it, still with dread, she decided that what he had done was a perfectly reasonable thing. She had invaded the servants' quarters, the only place they could call their own. And he had punished her painfully, though not dangerously. And—

Imbecile! Blanch called herself.

The costume of the child, the butler's sideburns, were all wrong. And there had been no staff during the few years she had lived there as a toddler.

Silly. She hadn't gotten herself a glass of water. Didn't want one now. She must justify her movements, if only to herself. She heard the truck driving off. From the great hall she could hear voices upstairs. She returned to the kitchen. There was no jam jar.

Had she seen the jar as a tot? As the child Blanch? She opened a cabinet, saw dozens of such jars. She ran the water for some time. The bustle of the kitchen. The cooks and assistant cooks. She must stop this. But they were there. She looked hard at the jam jar and it became a jam jar, and the water was good, as Shoreham water always was.

Enough for the morning, she would lunch.

The main door was open. She left it open, walked straight down the center of the great lawn. She stopped in the center and sat down. The lawn party was livelier than ever. White canvas shoes and flapper skirts. Cloches, bobs. The other kids saw her and came running toward her. She struggled, the horizon canted, righted itself, she was alone.

I shall have to stop it.

When she returned to her home, Tod's brother was there with his wife and two infants.

"We have a conference in Boston and I thought I'd show Caroline the Cape."

It was nice seeing Randolph, who practiced in Ohio.

Edna had been hard-put to entertain them.

"We're taking you to lunch," Randolph said. "Where's a good place?"

"Nowhere. Honestly."

"Then we'll go to a pretentious one."

Edna declined. Aaron wasn't consulted.

The children were sunny.

At the inn, when Caroline took them to wash up, Randolph said, "You look good. Your recovery is remarkable, though to be expected of a young healthy person. But something's troubling you."

"It's not Tod," Blanch said. "I'm working in this strange, darned house, the estate you saw as you came to our place. It used to belong to my mother and my mother's folks, and their folks. And I'm getting time hallucinations, sort of *déjà vu*'s."

"That big stuccoed thing."

"Yes."

"Again not unusual. I think I would too. But should that trouble you so much?"

"Am I that troubled?"

He waited, as though expecting her to say more.

Finally he urged, "There's nothing more?"

That drawing-down within her. Though it hadn't occurred for a while. She wouldn't. She would. She started to tell him, and then it was pointless, the great crystal star before her, the halting of her speech.

He was there, but barely there. Caroline returned with the children. All Ohioans, nice peo-

ple. Not even related. Descending the steps of
the porch, she had to hold the rail. What interest
had they? And what could they know?

She could see the thinness of their smiles now.
Not superficial, just formal. They parted on
a "You-must-see-us-when-you're-in-our-neck-of-the
woods" level. The children were cute cubs. All
plastic.

Again on the great curved driveway to the big
house, the sun and the lawn hers, she found her
walk easy and vibrant as ever.

Wow! Randolph marveled. Either the biggest
built-in monitor ever! Or snob!

THEY HAD driven all the way down to Hyannis,
for a movie, but first ate at the Mayflower.

Blanch told Milan about her recent delusions.
"On condition you don't decide I'm a nut."

She knew he wouldn't, and he didn't.

"You could leave. I wish you'd quit."

But then it turned out she did, and then didn't,
need the money.

"Well I think the trouble is that you like it."

"What?"

"The hallucinations."

"No I don't think I do."

"Then why not just stop going there?"

"Because— Because they seem to be related.
They all seem to be part of the same big thing."

"But you've been calling them delusions and

hallucinations. That's not very sane."

"I know."

"Then isn't that enough?"

"To run away from?"

"Let's say to avoid. To have nothing to do with them."

"But first I want to tie them all together."

"That looks like a dangerous game."

"Then what shall I do?"

"Quit. At least for a while."

"I'll go to New York for a week."

She could see that Milan would miss her.

SHE PHONED a friend with whom she had gone to both Greenbrier and Jackson.

Gloria said, "Jeez, the folks are in Europe and I'm booked for the Orient. But the apartment's yours and the key's at the desk."

Blanch thanked her. She was sorry that she would not see Gloria, but suspected that it would be better to be alone.

"What are you doing?"

"I'm playing with ghosts."

"No kidding?!"

Blanch laughed. Might as well let it out. In fact it was fun talking, first with Randolph, then with Milan, whom she had wanted to talk to, but hadn't dared to until after Randolph. And now Gloria.

Blanch's silly diffidence. Thanks to poor Edna and Aaron.

It was surprising how amusing the encounters sounded, as she told them to her former room-mate.

Gloria was enthralled, said, "How do you do it?"

"Oh, I seem to be popping into different worlds and times."

"Hey, that's a riot!"

"I'll have to tell you more about it some time."

"Yes, do—at another time! I've got to go. We'll have to get together."

How quick and easy it had been to cut herself off from Manhattan. Had she ever lived there?

For that matter, had she ever lived anywhere?

She had been taken from the big house as a tot, was not sure that she remembered anything, although she seemed to recall wicker furniture and reed carpets. Then they had lived in a rented house in Shoreham. Only old people lived in the adjoining houses—in fact, it seemed, all through town. And a dangerous highway before the house.

And then boarding schools, including that awful place in Switzerland. It had been depressing, and Blanch wondered how Edna eventually found out that it more or less specialized in wealthy retardees, and got her out.

As a tot Blanch had been so subject to poison ivy and allergies (which, as soon as she believed they were psychosomatic, disappeared) that she was spared camps.

And then college, and then Manhattan.

Living in the mid-Sixties, Madison Avenue area, there were the hurried and rarely pleasant meals in crowded, not-too-cheap restaurants, and the prohibitive distance to grocery stores—which were expensive, and carried weird brand names. And the megalopolitan slots for living, working, play—vertical, with small doors to the narrow streets. A cold, hard area, though elegant. She might have liked Greenwich Village, she might have liked Central Park and the Metropolitan Museum of Art. They weren't far from where she lived. But wherever she went there was the after-taste of her absurdly small and costly room, and the hardness of asphalt and concrete around her.

This was better, Gloria's place was just around the corner from Central Park.

It was a dark day with glistening pavements, the bushes and trees and buildings dressed in fog, the red and green stop lights, and the amber and brake lights of the cars, alive. She really felt posh as she dismissed the cab, turned the corner to the town house in which Gloria's folks had an apartment, the world falling away, the rain like slanting halo bars over her sealskin coat, the lions beside the entrance writhing just for her, above the door Neptune, and on each side of him two strong-faced bas-relief heads shaping their classic lips at her, bulging their strong eyes.

She rang for the butler and didn't ring, pushing open the outer door, distressed by what the rain and muck had done to her loafers (Or had they been that tacky when she started?) and the soaking that it had given her thin jacket that had been enough when she left Shoreham.

It was no longer a town house, but a row of town houses attached to one larger new building, all entered through this lobby with its doorman, who was hiding from the rain; the complex a sort of horizontal skyscraper.

The living room had a row of windows with a cattycorner view of the park. The buildings opposite were grey and comforting.

Living in some one else's place was always a drag. One could resist and feel churlish, or succumb and feel like a poor relation.

To camp or take over?

Blanch hung and placed her things where she could.

In looking for cream she found the huge refrigerator-freezer full of gourmet treats, with a handwritten note inside folded to stand, and reading:

> Think of me as you get fat—use any of the booze but Dad's Napoleon brandy.
>
> Gloria!

Blanch decided that she knew no one closer than Gloria. Yet, as she recalled, they had hardly ever been together, their relationship had been

one of Blanch doing all sorts of things to cover
Gloria's absences, latenesses, holidays from home
when she was one place and supposed to be
elsewhere. And all of it absurdly innocent, and
especially since Gloria's divorced and remarried
parents and their lawyers hadn't really cared.
Blanch's advantage was having their room all to
herself for weekends and holidays.

Blanch felt like a pig eating frozen lobster
thermidore and drinking a tiny bottle of cham-
pagne; decided she would get fat if she weren't
careful.

She gasped as she returned to the drawing room
to find Paxton standing against the windows. Silent and intent, his powerful shoulders and arms
in shirtsleeves, in the striped vest he wore when
cleaning, or putting the finish to cleaning. He
was carefully dusting and polishing bibelots, little statues and things, he had just finished one
of the sets but had not put it away. There was
something fearsome in the arrogance of his not
turning, he knew she was there, no one stole up
on Paxton. And it was nonsense, it wasn't Paxton,
for there was no, never had been a Paxton for
her. Anyway, she wasn't that afraid of Paxton,
though she was fearful of the person it probably
or truly was.

And then she exclaimed with a sigh. The fog,
the darkness, had lifted, it was brighter, and what
she had seen was the butler at the window across
the narrow street, busily dusting Meissen and
Royal Doulton figurines. Elegant, but not Paxton.

What Paxton?

Blanch had to caution herself that she was supposed to be getting away from all that.

The rain had stopped. She strolled up Fifth Avenue, a thoroughfare on which no men make passes. Then she found herself imperious at the top of the steps of one of the last great mansions, before the incredulous eyes of a private policeman.

She wilted, turned, descended.

"Hey lady!" he called.

She hurried away, humiliated by the people who may have seen that brief exchange, that absurd moment, with the carriages jammed and waiting, and the uniformed footmen from the back of a chaise giving her a condescending leer. Even the horses clopping by, thoroughbreds and hackneys, seemed amused. Busses, cars jammed. Horses! This was absurd. Suddenly, for the first time, Blanch was profoundly terrified.

Was she withdrawing into insanity? Or—the idea just as insane—sliding back into another era from which she could not return?

Decide today how you would handle a dinosaur. Tomorrow may be too late.

Shut up!

Absurd.

Edith Wharton and her New York were all right for the American novel. But this was too much. She was afraid to look up, look around her, afraid that the pavement beneath her loafers, thank heavens they were still loafers, would turn to mud, with sweepers at the crossings. Did Manhattan ever have crossing sweepers? She would have to ask Gloria on her next visit. Ha!

She hurried to the most modern theater she could think of, on Lexington in the Fifties, saw a film made in today's Zurich, and was grimly amused to see that although time was not violated, truth was, with lots of things happening or perhaps not happening, and was somewhat pleased to find the ending go to pot with some sort of reasonable tying-together of the strands, though the Perhaps still remained Perhaps.

Viva Zurich! Viva the new cinema!

As she was leaving the lobby, a girl who had sat near her, who had been in the theater before Blanch but had not left until Blanch did, came up to her. The small girl had thick unruly hair and an unbecoming, unfashionable print dress, large desperately hungry eyes, and a smile so fearful of rejection that Blanch could almost cry. She said, "I live in the Lexington Avenue YWCA, would you? I mean could you if it's on your way walk me there? I mean we could walk together."

Blanch was touched, suddenly wondered if she herself dared to walk to Gloria's place. It was on the way.

"Let's have a coffee first."

Dismay further flooded the girl's features. "I don't—"

"I'm buying."

As they had coffee the girl asked Blanch what

she thought of the film. Before Blanch could reply, she gave an encyclopedic account of the filmmaker's career and methods, then shifted to remarks about Zurich, with dates.

Blanch could see why she was so lonely.

The girl kept talking, swiftly, pedantically, compulsively as they walked to the Y. At the entrance the girl asked, desperately and as though expecting to be rebuffed, if they might meet again, there was a wonderful series of poetry readings at the YMHA.

"I'm leaving tomorrow morning," Blanch said.

She started for Gloria's. It was night, with Lexington Avenue oddly empty of cars at so early an hour.

Three hippy-looking youths hurried toward her from a side street. Insecure, she flagged a cab. As she got in she saw that they were divinity students in shirtsleeves, with reversed collars.

You lose a little, you gain a little.

The next morning was sunny. She dropped into the offices of *Rise: "The Bright Teenager's Guide to the Future."* Whatever it started out as, it was now a middling success as a gleaner of advertising for young male and female togs and anti-acne cosmetics. She would say hello to the gang.

Just inside the door there was *angst* and hysteria, and Mr. Morgenblut yelling, skittering between cubicles, "Della, Stella and Sheila are on vacation, the two new ones are sick, so please don't socialize and ask about money yet, just get to the layout room and give a hand, you look fine and at least for a couple of days it won't kill you."

Sabetha the receptionist winked and looked pretty-please. Blanch went to the layout room. A shaggy flower child looked at her.

"Throw me out if you want to," Blanch said. "I worked here for months and Mr. Morgenblut begged me to pitch in for a few days."

"Then you know how it is?"

"That I do."

Risha and she were soon working smoothly together.

At three Mr. Morgenblut came in with coffee and tuna fish salad sandwiches, shouting as he glanced at the layouts, "You're angels, you're darlings but I want you should be more psychologically favoring the major and more consistent accounts," his tone wrenched between thanking and browbeating.

The flower child gave him a muted, ladylike Bronx cheer which he disregarded as he turned and left.

"And I just thought I'd drop in and say hello," Blanch said.

The door opened and Mr. Morgenblut said, "Time enough for lunch, we must get the work done soon."

"Coming back?" said Risha.

"Since nothing's changed, I doubt it."

Though it was fun.

They did a remarkable amount of work that day and the next morning.

At one point during lunch Risha said, "I don't know how I could live with all those servants. I mean I feel that all people are beautiful. But I want to touch them. And I don't know how that would work out at all."

What had occasioned that remark?

Blanch watched Risha curiously, who went on, "I mean, I don't begrudge it, with your regattas and—"

"My what?"

"I mean, I've seen kids with money, though nothing like you're talking about. And somehow it seems so old-fashioned. You know, square and creepy."

Lord! What had Blanch been saying?

"Don't get me wrong. I think you're cool. But I couldn't take two weeks off, especially this time of year. And you got to have clothes for things like that."

That dreadful pulling from below, as though a hand had reached up through a crack in the floor, as though it were deep in her intestines, or groping her pancreas and lungs—not painful, but drawing down, psychically painful in its persistence. But she would fight it.

With difficulty Blanch said, "How was I acting? When I said what I said?"

Risha looked worried, but Blanch wanted to know.

"I don't know. I mean, friendly. But uppity, cold. Since you asked, I'd say snotty. You know. Plastic polite—you're not—?"

"It's complicated," Blanch said. Her vitality

had suddenly resurged, drumming in her, her body, her face, charged.

"Like this head butler—"

"Excuse me."

Blanch grabbed her purse and rushed out.

Morgenblut confronted her in the foyer.

"You're leaving?" he instantly sensed.

"I've got to go."

"You won't re—"

"No."

"Then let me pay you and nag you—"

"Send it—"

"Here's fifty, no here's sixty dollars—this way there's no tax or social security—"

"You're a doll goodbye—"

"I hope you always come in even if you don't work permanent—"

She left him speaking in the foyer.

She would have to get back to Shoreham fast. It had come with her, whatever it was.

She was never one to take things lying down. As an only child she had always had to hold her own, she prided herself on surrendering to no one person or thing.

But she was furious with herself, felt it was a mess that the whole thing had started, that perhaps she might have avoided it. If she had refused to work in the big house? Or turned the job down as soon as things began to happen? Yet she suspected that there had been previous indications.

Now she was scared, maybe more angry than scared, at the suspicion that the only way to stop what had been happening to her was to get lots of questions answered, and that could only be done at Shoreham.

She packed what little she had, left a note to the maid who was supposed to come once a week and left a thank-you note for Gloria. But even while she was writing the notes, and later, purchasing the bus ticket, she felt that her voice was not her own, nor her hands.

By the time she entered the bus, the only link to Shoreham, she still felt determined. But also frightened, with a ringing nervous terror accelerating her respiration, heartbeat, raising her blood pressure, stimulated by the threat of losing her personality, whatever that was, a little something she was at least comfortable in, called Blanch Stowe. And then the dread of the other personality—or identity, or possession—whatever it was—filtering into her mind, perhaps body, and taking over. This enemy a superior, upper-class thing with its mansion and grounds, and used to having servants, now seemed to be both her and not her, but on the verge of totally taking over. How awful that she might become a dream—and not much of a dream at that—and It become the reality.

She turned ashen at the recollection of a television study dealing with insanity. At one point a teenager retrieved from madness for a time by chemical or electric therapy, learned that her return was temporary, that she was sliding back into perpetual mindlessness. The incident was not staged and as the camera, through a one-way window, recorded her hopelessness, her agony, tears and valid self-pity, Blanch, suffering for and with the pitiful girl, was thankful in the thought that this would never be her lot. Now she was terrified.

MR. MALLKIN had been suspiciously quick to oblige concerning her vacation (Was her work that unnecessary?) but now seemed eager to have her back.

"Your stay was less than you suggested."

"I couldn't wait to get back."

"I have never had a great affection for Manhattan."

It had been fun returning to this big old house, her fears suddenly allayed, as though the scare had merely been a subconscious urge to return. The empty great hall, the refectory—though there, something had been added. A huge U-shaped banquet table, slabs of plywood on metal folding legs. But the house retained the emptiness, despite the bright linens and unlit candles, awaiting the dinner party, the intricately folded napkins and

STOP!

There were no linens, candles, napkins. Just the bare tables. So temporary, so unpeopled.

smooth or polished surface is of itself a good protection, polished tin or Russia iron having a ratio, for radiation, of 53 to 100

Someone walked behind her. She would not turn.

She typed on. It stood behind her. Paxton? Absurd.

Light footed. Walking to one end of the room and back, behind her. He hadn't entered by the door. She turned.

The young yachtsman stopped, smiled at her.

"Hello," she said.

"Hello." His the sweetest, shyest smile, and wall of separation. He screamed money.

"The Cape's lovely today, isn't it?"

He smiled. "It is."

"Indeed it is," said the little man with the bald dome, coming through the door.

The yachtsman could have come through the door too, Blanch hadn't been looking. And then the open window behind her.

"It's very different from Mexico, where we've just spent months. Isn't it different from Mexico, Hugh?" the old man said.

"Yes, it's different." Loving. The smile. He seemed to have all the time in the world.

"But we mustn't disturb her, we must leave her for a treatment, mustn't we, Hugh?"

Smiling, Hugh left.

"I'll see you upstairs in a moment, Hugh." To Blanch: "It's really disgusting the way the allopaths restrict us homeopaths, ban us like mad dogs."

"It is rather one-sided when you think of it," said Blanch. "Like cutting something off before it's really been given a chance."

The chiropractor beamed, then looked even stiffer and more professional.

"You must let me give you a treatment sometime. Just between us. And of course there won't be regular fees."

"Thank you," said Blanch.

"Oh the exasperation he gives me, and how little she's paying me," the chiropractor complained; "I'm sort of retired you know, not practicing. I *can't* practice here with those sharks," and left.

Not much typing at this rate.

Mr. Mallkin came bustling in. "Did you see him? The young man—"

"Hugh? He's upstairs with the—doctor."

"Doctor? Oh. —Unfortunate boy. Unfortunate boy."

A phone rang from beyond, probably upstairs. Blanch hadn't thought of one being in the house, somehow.

"It's nothing, it's nothing," Mallkin said, leaving.

So far as Blanch was concerned.

She'd started late, but supposed she would lunch.

The sun was a wall of brightness. She felt sleek and golden. The door to the north outbuilding was open—not opening, open. She hadn't seen those movements lately. She looked back. She had left the main door open, the masses of windows were open. How sunny and pleasant everything was.

At Aaron and Edna's the phone was ringing. It was Mallkin, sounding distressed.

"Could you see going to Hyannis and picking up a small parcel at the bus depot? You have access to a car? I'll pay you for your time of course, and the mileage. Go immediately so you won't be late. Enjoy yourself there. But you must be there on time, it's the Boston bus. Otherwise it will just lie about the bus depot. It's addressed to me."

"I have a car."

She drove to Milan's place. He was washing the breakfast dishes.

"Courier service. I'm supposed to pick up a package in Hyannis. I am to start 'far too early so that nothing can delay mine errand.' Going with me?"

"Swell. Want to pick up some art supplies."

In the car Milan said, "You're back early."

Blanch had forgotten, almost amused she said, "I was chased back."

"You seem fine now."

"I am."

"Chased?"

"I don't quite remember now why. I suppose I don't want to remember. Maybe I could if I try. But I know one thing. I want to fight. And I think I'll have to win here."

There was nothing to see but sand hills and their low, dark covering plants.

"Is there a lot of that? Not wanting to remember?" He asked very gently. Milan by his tone seemed to be conveying that he was neither guiding nor chiding her, merely curious.

"I don't think it's tragic or anything. What should one want to remember?"

Milan looked gentler than ever.

WHEN THEY returned from Hyannis, Milan drove, though it was Edna's car, directly to the door of the big house. There were lights in the attic and shrieks and yowls. With the door open, the bellowing, the wolflike howls, became incredible. Blanch looked toward Milan and shrugged. Milan left the car and joined her in the great hall. They stood there, (Blanch with the package in her hand) the shrieks and scuffles and muffled curses continuing above.

Milan slammed the door, smashed the sole of his sneaker several times against it. The noise was impressive, brought silence above. Then a thin wail and the sound of walking, and Mr. Mallkin at the railing above.

Blanch trotted up the stairs and handed him the package.

"Thank you so much. This is most distressing," he said. "You're coming tomorrow?"

Blanch nodded, but stayed near the top of the steps.

Mr. Mallkin said, "A most unfortunate boy. We're trying to help him. Thank you again and you must forgive me."

Milan looked curious.

"It looks like a rich nut," Blanch said, descending the steps.

Milan didn't seem impressed with the explanation. Then said, "It seems to stop the other things."

Blanch had to laugh, unbelievingly. "But this is so mad!" And to herself, *"What am I doing here?"*

They'd eaten lunch together, she refused dinner with him, drove Milan to his cabin.

"And now you're going to work all night?"

"You bet," he smiled.

But he watched her retreating car until he could see it no longer.

SHE RECOILED when she put on the light in her room. The black crystal star lay on her bed.

With lips drawn Blanch went down to Edna's room, knocked on the door.

"You may come in."

Edna sat in her small upholstered chair reading *The Christian Science Monitor.*

"Yes?"

Blanch's determination left her. How could you query her? Feebly, though ostensibly evenly, she heard herself say, "Were you in my room?"

"I haven't been above stairs for days."

"Aaron?"

"I'm sure not."

But of course no question of why.

"May I sit?"

"Yes."

"There are so many things I don't know."

Edna waited. Humorless, concerned.

"What was mother like?"

Edna thought for some time. At last said, "She was the daughter of moneyed people, reared in their milieu."

That was supposed to do.

"You weren't close?"

"I never tried to influence"—she had difficulty in uttering the next word—"them in any way. We had expected Benjamin to enter social service, either here or internationally."

The last showed what had separated son and parents. If it had.

"Then what did mummy and daddy (Had she ever said those words before?) —my mother and father—do?"

"To my knowledge, the only thing one can say they did is travel, extensively."

Blanch knew enough to know what Edna was not saying—that their travel was not as travel, but only a means to get them to the luxurious places in which they idled. They were lost in a typhoon on the Indian Ocean.

"Did I ever see the big house when it was at its peak?"

Edna waited.

"I mean, with its elaborate furniture?"

"The house was stripped in 1929. That was well before you were born."

Edna waited.

Blanch would have liked Edna to tell about her son, Benjamin, what he looked like, what he said, and if Edna was as scrupulously honest—and cold—to him as she was to Blanch.

"Thank you," said Blanch.

Edna sat silent, waiting for her to leave, her intense, peering, analyzing, pleasureless eyes on her. One could never forget that Edna was totally, endlessly concerned with the plight of every deprived child, starving nation, ugly prison system, as well as, Blanch felt, Blanch's own doubts, unhappiness; and sad herself in the belief that there was nothing she, Edna, really could do about them. There was love but no humor, no affection, which is a form of humor. Perhaps that was it, that was the most important thing in the world, humor, even more than love, because only that could unlock love. But Blanch felt that if she ran up to Edna now and kissed her, rumpled her hair, it would only be an assault, with grave-faced Edna being jostled, and bearing it, and watching intently as though she would like to please Blanch, and knowing that it was hopeless; all must die, all must suffer, we are helpless in this net of chance.

Blanch hardly noticed Aaron sitting in his chair at the living room window holding a book in his hand, the heft of it in his right hand, the cover and flyleaf resting on his left.

She stepped into the night. It was balmy.

Stars.

The star. The black crystal star. She could have removed it in getting a slip from her drawer. After making the bed?

She strolled to the highway. Where does one walk? She walked the length of the front, low brick wall to the entrance, walked in, along the semicircle of tarmac. The big house was dark, all the windows closed. Someone stood before the main door, in a white shirt with a pale dome, then the glow of a cigar.

"Good evening."

Blanch stopped.

"He's quiet now. He's from Philadelphia. His mother is very wealthy. She doesn't pay me at all enough to take care of him. I sold my things and apartment and everything. Cut all my ties. What she pays me is a pittance."

"That's unfortunate," Blanch said.

He said no more, went into the darkened house.

One could understand how troubled he was.

Blanch walked on. In a way she had owned this once. The pavement beneath her had belonged to her. And as aware as she was of the triviality of ownership, where even our lives are a usufruct, things on loan, as it were, that would eventually be withdrawn, returned, ended, she could not help feeling an arrogance of ownership. The feeling of possession, of being at home, grew, was warm; certainly better than that utterly bleak "new" shingled house she was living in. As she passed the south outbuilding, companion and double to the one north of the big house, she heard and almost immediately saw Mr. Mallkin in the doorway.

"What did he say to you? Forgive the question, it's not idle. What did he say to you?"

Blanch paused, spoke. "That the boy's mother is from Philadelphia and that he isn't being paid enough by her."

"He didn't say anything about me, anything?"

"No, Mr. Mallkin."

"Life is so full of sad things when things should be amusing and elegant and cheery, don't you think? One does what one can. But I'll bet you are merry," he said grudgingly, then with a laugh, "I'll bet you are merry."

Of all the silly things. Blanch had to laugh.

"You are a philosopher."

"But a gay one, a gay one. You're going for a walk, I see."

"Yes."

"Merry, merry," he said. "Don't let me stop your—peregrination."

Blanch took the hint.

Real little community of pals.

But things had been better since she'd returned. Perhaps everything was going to be all right. It was a lovely night.

WHAT AN immense amount of typescript. None of which she understood. Promptly, on Friday mornings, she found her pay for the previous week, for the endless typing of the incomprehensible. As for the page number, she only knew it from the last part-sheet she always seemed to leave. The money was in cash, only her name was written on the envelope, and the amount.

She startled. She'd hardly noticed it before. It was not the handwriting of the manuscript. Another one of the mysteries.

Mr. Mallkin looked in.

"Thank you again," Blanch said.

"It is I who benefit."

"I wonder—?"

"Yes?"

"The Bay porch. May I visit it sometimes?"

"The Bay porch—ah yes, the Bay porch. You may visit—the Bay porch."

Which sounded pretty much as though that was all she had better visit.

But Mr. Mallkin was not the one to end anything decisively.

"Such a lovely sweater," he said. "You are a pleasant face in an otherwise desert."

Hmph!

Mr. Mallkin's face had fallen into a vapid smile, though his eyes were wary. Covertly wary, but wary.

Blanch looked him straight in the eye, to see that he wasn't at the door, that she was alone.

UH UH!

Blanch arose and stepped to the side, to see through the refectory to the main hall. A shapely woman, in peasant blouse and dirndl, and carrying a coat, started up the grand stairs and passed Blanch's line of vision.

Thrilling and haunting, like a splash in a silent mountain pool. A dark pool.

Visitors.

"I WOULD certainly not presume to tell you which friend is sincere and which not."

Richard smiled across his broad, honest face.

"But you just did."

"Of that I was not aware."

"By being you."

Blanch tried to stifle her blush, could have screamed at the blush she knew that she could not stifle. Yet had to laugh. He was such an outright devil.

"Isn't there a matter of—gender—involved?" The blood thrilled in her veins.

"Forgive me. I merely meant elegance and grace beside—"

"Disgrace, I would say."

"All right."

"Then how could you have?"

"I felt that he was more to be pitied than censured."

How Christian of Richard, struggling so bravely to snatch his poor friend Dennis from both "the enemy grape" and that *person*. How noble. And women were supposed to be finer.

"But don't you feel that the *missionary* might be in peril?"

His fine brow darkened.

"That is something for which one must be on the alert."

Hester, his sister, called to him.

"I'm afraid, Blanch, that we must leave."

"I still suspect that you may be very naughty."

Richard didn't take that as negatively as he should. Suddenly there was a chill. For him too?

"Until we meet soon?"

Blanch smiled, a qualified, contingent smile. They—she—had just been rather rash.

He tipped his hat as they drove off, smartly flicking the reins.

Blanch nodded slightly.

And Paxton was there, close to her, supervising the removal of the tea things and having the tables brought in, too close to her, not looking a day older than when she was a tot, a loyal guardian, an irreplaceable arbiter, yet more presumptuously self-assured daily. And if it weren't that the staff needed a heavy hand, she would have asked mother to remove him.

Nothing was simple.

In the conservatory she reached for her Tauch-nitz edition, and her face turned ashen. The light was grey, it was late, almost six. Where had she been that whole day? Or rather, she knew, both currently and, presumably, in the past. But Blanch Stowe did not recall getting up, dressing, eating, going to work, spending the day at work. Had she lunched? And was it right to lose, say, seven hours, for a fragment of an exchange at the end with those two dead people? Or was this, her current self, the lost time? Was being Blanch Stowe, living on the Cape, typing for Mr. Mall-kin, a loss of time for that other Blanch?

That was her mother's name, Blanch, too. But Richard's flat straw hat, his high collar, tight pants, big suitcoat. That might have been grand-ma's period—1920? No. 1900. That would have been great-great-grandmother's time. And yet Blanch had seen them, that is, the same women, in cloches, which was absurd, for those were the tight felt hats of 1928, at most a little earlier. The time sphere, or at least the fragment of time, the scenes, seemed to be getting all mixed up, which made Blanch wonder if she were actually any-body, any one person.

And where was the fight for her identity that she had returned from Manhattan to wage? Then she had thought she was going to have to fight out of one time period in which her "enemy" lived. Now it looked as though there were whole loops of time developing, like coils of barbed wire, and perhaps there was more than one identity that she would have to fight.

She slipped into her jacket, at the door of the main hall decided to stop on the Bay porch for a moment. She ran up the steps, the halls were indeed barren, stepped through the glass door, stiffened. The lovely lady she had seen the day before stood at the railing, looking out over the water. There was a peace and aestheticism in this lone figure.

Treading lightly Blanch went to the railing.

Really something. What a difference a few feet of elevation made. And the billowing clouds, the red sunset.

She stole a glance to her left and winced.

The woman's legs were young, shapely and sturdy, her figure good, with her thin peasant blouse and soft, clinging dirndl. But she wore nothing under them that Blanch could see. Her face was carved of rock, and she had no teeth, merely a deep, jagged notch in her profile. She turned and looked at Blanch. Her eyes were black and violent. Blanch thought that the strange woman was about to say something to her, but instead she looked through her, seemed to break her and cast her aside with a venomous look, or completely discard her as flotsam, as a weak enemy.

Blanch turned and retreated from the porch. Never had she seen such hammer-forged hardness.

At home Milan was waiting for her. As soon as she entered, Edna left.

"You've been having a chat!"

As they left, for fried clams and coffee, Milan said, "Believe it or not, yes. She asked me what I thought about the mess in Rumania and Czechoslovakia. I told her I didn't know. But she seemed so eager, I told her what I guess things are like there."

"Fantastic. But she didn't say anything?"

Milan laughed. "No, not really."

Blanch told him what had happened that day, about her not recalling anything.

"I think you've got to see a specialist. It could be very serious."

"I still think I'm more mad than scared."

"But you're intelligent. And there must be people who specialize in such things."

"Are you sure?"

"But you've just got to do something."

"This is terrifying," Blanch admitted. "But I feel that if they can do anything, it can wait. And if they can't—why go?"

"Well I'm certainly not qualified to say anything," Milan said hopelessly. "But you've got to do something."

"I've got to fight it out here," Blanch said determinedly.

It was painful for Milan. "Then if you don't intend to see anyone, why do you tell me?" This was not a protest but a plea.

"It is rotten," Blanch admitted. "It's only that I thought you could tell me if I really needed help."

"What about now?"

"I mean, if I couldn't communicate at all."

Her logic, without seeming to satisfy him, seemed to stop him.

Hurt. "Don't say such things!" But he nodded assent.

She tried to smile her thanks to him, appreciated what he had just said. For he was becoming involved, though neither of them was committed in any way.

The perfect union. It amused her—amused her as much as she could be, walking dangerously on the fence of fear that separated her from the zero of that whole day of her not knowing where she had been, but suspecting.

Another fear tugged at her mind. Did she want to be in this thing, this other world, as an escape from the hopelessness of Shoreham? What had she done with her young life when it was fully hers?

Milan broke into her thoughts, said, "Well, since we're in it together, then I'm going to do a little spying of my own. What about dropping around to the big house tonight?"

"What do you expect to find?"

"Nothing."

"Okay," Blanch said.

The moon was ragged and dirty, brown and white, with very little light reaching the ground. Which seemed odd because there was light on the Bay.

They parked on the road to Edna and Aaron's place, then hurried to the big house, stopped at the sight of perhaps twenty cars parked in the driveway, with several on the road.

"Big doings at the house," Blanch said, then recalled the new table set up in the refectory.

Silently Milan walked along the wall behind the north outbuildings, stopped at the end, where there was an open space before they came to the big house.

He clutched her arm. It was the first time he had ever touched her.

"Here goes," he said.

Both stooping, they ran the distance, crouched outside the conservatory. The chandeliers burned, a muddy brown light. Still crouching, they both slowly looked up and in.

There was a giant, in his fifties, with curly blond hair (a wig or dyed?), with him a small, elegant man, both in casual clothes. They seemed to be demonstrating something to three other men, all short and fine featured and tense, the first two holding out their hands and stepping back, then raising an arm and stepping forward. There was much talk, one laughed. The tall blond, who had a bulldog face, seemed to get very angry. The others seemed in awe of him.

Because the window was shut, Milan and Blanch could hear nothing.

Milan, followed by Blanch, walked stooping to the refectory windows.

The room was alive with light, the long tables covered with linen, either tablecloths or bed sheets, almost reaching the floor; gay with varie-

gated candelabra. The room was jammed with
several dozen men standing in groups, talking
and laughing. There was a youthfulness of clothes
though not of age, the wearers running from dyed
hair or wigged sixties to tired young men in their
twenties, all with a fineness of features, a smooth-
ness of face, either red or pale, some with distin-
guished-looking tans. Gales of speech came
through the open windows and from the open
door to the hall.

"Quite a party!"

"Or meeting," Milan said.

He nodded to the doorway ahead. They walked
by very quickly, passing men in the great hall.
The room on the other side was concealed behind
drawn window shades. They passed that, again
reached an open space, this time next to the
south outbuildings.

Two burly figures burst from behind them,
confronted Milan and Blanch.

"Where do you think you're going?"

"We were just walking."

"I think you'd better come with us."

"We were just strolling."

"We think you'd better come with us."

Milan looked them over. At last he laughed.

"I think you've convinced me," he said off-
handedly, turned, took Blanch's arm and they
walked to the house.

As they approached, the massive figure of Mr.
Mallkin came to the door.

"Hi," Blanch said.

"We were just strolling by and these two guys invited us in," Milan said. He had met Mallkin when they delivered the package from Hyannis.

"Oh? Busy busy," said Mr. Mallkin. "I don't know if you'll find it interesting. But make the house your own." He turned and hurried into the refectory.

The two who had accosted them didn't look as formidable inside, now appeared as puffy, officious spoiled brats. Although they did, Blanch felt, save face by the schooled coolness and arrogance with which they stared through Milan and her before ambling into the south room.

Milan grinned at Blanch, shrugged. They went into the refectory.

There was a great din of talk, with place names bandied about—Ibiza, L.A., Acapulco, the Village—as well as hotel names and those of mutual acquaintances.

Milan looked at Blanch for orders. She smiled and nodded toward the door. The men seemed to be busy not looking at Blanch, but quickly appraising Milan.

As they left the refectory they passed the chiropractor, who turned away.

"Come on!" she whispered. Once in the great hall, she trotted up the stairs. Milan followed.

The long corridor was dimly lit by small, yellowing bulbs. The doors of some of the rooms were open. In these the light was bright, dropping oblongs of illumination into the hall. They looked into several rooms. In each there were metal cots and luggage on the floor. There were no bureaus.

"This is really thrilling," Milan kidded.

"It was your idea."

One door was locked. There was a thin line of light at its base. Milan peeked through the ancient keyhole, nodded Blanch to it.

She crouched, could see someone sitting at a window opposite the door, his face dazed, his irises pinpoints. It was Hugh. And then a blur, a woman's hand touching his head, and then the midriff of the woman of the Bay porch approaching the door.

Panicky, Blanch ran into the nearest lighted doorway, Milan following. They stood against the wall.

They heard Hugh's door unbolted, opened, then after a pause, shut and bolted again.

Milan glanced into the hall, then looked at Blanch, who waved at him to follow her and rushed on light feet to the end of the corridor, then up to the servants' quarters.

Several rooms were lighted here, too. Fears of Paxton catching her again rippled up and down her back. The ceiling seemed so much lower now than when she was a child. There was nothing to see, except for the great Bay outside. They returned to the second floor, went out on the Bay porch.

Below they could hear and see the people on the terrace. All terribly eager and reminiscent and general.

"What are we looking for?" Milan said.

"I don't know."

"I'm still glad I thought of it. I feel better."

Blanch agreed. Knowledge is power. Maybe.

Again in the hall, they met two men coming up the stairs, who paused, regarded them.

"Hm!" said one as they parted, each going to a separate room.

Several stood in the great hall.

When Blanch and Milan reached the bottom of the steps, Mallkin appeared from the south room, came up to them and said, "Leaving? So nice that you could come. So now you see the sort of thing we do here"—the only dig at their invasion. Urbane, lightning fast in the minuscule pause to let it sink in, yet all the more chilling for that. "Come any time, both of you, you're always welcome. Joy, joy," he closed, and returned to the refectory.

Several men smiled perfunctorily at the departing couple.

Outside, in the light of the doorway, they encountered the two men who had caught them. They turned aside with frigid dignity.

Now Blanch and Milan walked down the driveway.

" 'We met an host and quelled it,' " Milan said.

"What?"

"I'm just quoting something."

"Oh. —I don't think it was a waste at all," Blanch said.

"It was interesting. The question is why? What did we expect to find?"

"It was nice of you," Blanch said.

"But I'm curious too."

"I mean—trying to keep it *outside of my self.*"

"Trying?" Then Milan laughed.

Blanch walked beside him, troubled, questioning. Was he mocking her?

Milan laughed again, said, "We're going in the wrong direction."

Blanch laughed too as they started back to the car.

There were the automobiles jammed along the driveway, there were a few cars moving along the highway, slowing down to gawk.

They reached the Dart.

"Let's go down to the Bay for a bit."

"Swell," said Blanch.

But they didn't go out onto the beach. Some distance directly in front of the big house a cross of candles was burning, flames dancing bravely in the breeze. Occasionally the flames would blink black. An illusion caused by figures walking by them.

"I think I've had it," Milan said.

"Me too," said Blanch.

THE NEXT morning the sky was leaden and low, the trees and shrubs seemed to be standing mute before expected punishment.

Blanch wondered if Mallkin had a car. It would be in one of the outbuildings.

Inside the house, the tables had been struck, the metal legs folded against them, the plywood sheets piled and leaning against the wall.

This was more like it, Blanch kidded herself.

And where and when had they gone, cars and all?

In the conservatory things were as they always were. Except—remarkable—the pile of manuscript she'd been whittling down, today seemed higher.

Suddenly there was a showerbath density of rain smashing outside. Now it was dark indeed.

Blanch flipped on the chandelier. The light was inadequate for typing.

She wrote a note in a big scrawl: NEED A DESK LAMP, and felt rather apologetic. She bunched it and threw it into the wastebasket, and wrote much more neatly:

> Paul, if you ever leave me in the lurch again the way you did I'll kill you. It may have been perfectly all right your going off in the boat with Madge, but imagine how it left me on the yacht with Benjamin, nobility and morality *oozing* out of his pores like poison out of a toad's warts. If he turns out to have an iota of gumption, I think I'll give you Madge. And this time it's going to take more than two cases to placate me. (Three cases?) Pig!
>
> Blanch

She looked over the handwriting in the dim light, and then the words.

She could have wept. Woebegone, she folded

the sheet of paper in four parts and placed it on the typewriter.

Again another Blanch had asserted herself.

Blanch Stowe found herself—it was not as though she were walking; it was as if her head were on some sort of a movie dolly—floating through the conservatory, the refectory, into the hall, the great hall, floating up the steps.

She was still she, Blanch Stowe, but something else was carrying her. There was no fear. If only, she hoped, this could be worked out mutually, rather than one succumbing to another.

In the hall she found herself walking toward Hugh's room.

Mr. Mallkin stepped out and said, "I wanted to see you— Oh, it's you!" then stopped speaking as Blanch came toward him. Then, "My dear Miss Stowe!"

"I hope you're finding your stay pleasant," Blanch said.

"I beg—"

"If you'd like for anything, ring for Paxton."

"I don't—"

"Come. You must have noticed. It is one of the prices we pay for service."

"Oh!" said Mr. Mallkin.

Blanch went to the south end of the hall, glanced at the great pot of hibiscus growing before the window.

There was a noise. She turned to her left.

Mr. Mallkin had vanished. The chiropractor had stepped out of his room.

"That's gratitude for you," he said. He was almost weeping.

Blanch waited.

"Hugh's gone. I suppose you don't know where he went."

"I don't," said Blanch, tottering between two worlds.

"He married that horrible woman. Did you see her? A corker, wasn't she? Now who in his right mind would marry a thing like that?"

Blanch didn't know what to say.

"I'm ruined, I've hit bottom. He was a morphine addict, you know. She's a nurse, she brought the drugs. What am I supposed to do now? I haven't got a thing."

This was terrible.

"I've broken all my ties. Even had my bench moved here at my own expense. That's real gratitude, isn't it?"

He rushed past her and hurried down the steps.

The south window—there were no flowers, no vase, no pedestal.

Blanch—was it two Blanches? Or three? Or four? She returned to the staircase.

Mr. Mallkin stood beside it, on the landing. Blanch didn't know how to respond, stopped a few steps down and turned.

Said, "Oh. Is there a lamp to type by?"

"Yes. Yes. I'll bring you one from my room."

She returned to the conservatory. It was almost night-dark. The rain was shattering, drumming, cascading past the windows. She typed for a while.

Suddenly the rain paused. She looked over the field. The butcher's wagon was leaving the grounds. The groundskeepers were working together, a man and two boys. There was such tranquility in this little dictatorship of Paxton's. Then the rain smashed again, came as a wall of moisture, and she was sitting again with Benjamin, the rain blowing in sheets, the anchored cabin cruiser bouncing on the churning waves.

A Quaker, he hadn't been in the war against the fascists, nor was he a conscientious objector, but he did seem to be an awfully decent sort, rather Lincolnesque, big muscled, big boned, with sharp features, better than that sleek runt Paul, and Blanch found herself writhing at these thoughts. It was not right. For this man was her— her—

> value is about equal to the same weight of pine wood, as it comes from the press

She was typing.

The rain was breaking, beginning to silver. Lighted rays somewhere. It was almost five. Perhaps the last of the sun. Whiter sheets. Not rain. Great films, different densities of paper, cellophane, shifting before her.

She donned her storm coat, slipped the hood over her hair. She turned off the desk lamp, the weak chandeliers.

Mr. Mallkin stood in the great hall.

"Guess that's all for today," Blanch said.

He looked at her worriedly, as though about to say something elaborate, then said, "Yes. Yes," and went into the south room.

She let herself out. In the short distance to her home the wetness soaked through her coat, blasted against her face, drenched her eyelashes.

She could see the Bay at the end of the road, steaming, pocked and churning. This was New England indeed, indeed.

As she approached her house, almost like walking under water, she saw women standing before it—two? three? four? She laughed, ran toward them. They weren't there. Variations in costume, rainware.

"*Apage mala vita*." Where had she seen that? "Out, awful somethingorother!"

She entered by the kitchen. Edna rushed to her, helped her take her wet things off.

Blanch had a small battery operated TV set. A compromise because Edna never watched television on the downstairs set unless it were a program dealing with world problems and well recommended by *The Monitor*.

After supper Blanch sat in her room, tried to watch TV, in fact, did, became relaxed to private-eye mysteries, to Westerns. She even watched one prime-time kiddy program. She may even have dozed off, awoke to a hand on her shoulder.

She turned, saw Paxton and screamed, Paxton holding her shoulder tight, looking down bitterly, his great knobby fingers digging into the velvet and ribbons of her dress. She heard Edna on the steps, tried to decide whether Paxton's eyes were passionate or satanic, turned to Edna.

"Gracious! What has happened?"

It was Blanch's turn to stare silently for a long time, then say, "Sorry. A nightmare."

Sure enough, she was lying on her coverlet.

Edna stood at the door, looking in and down at Blanch. So like Edna. Despite the smallness of the house, people didn't barge into each other's rooms. Or because of its smallness?

Blanch looked at Edna, not lovingly, but as questioningly, she was sure, as Edna looked at her. Absurd relationship. So different from Milan's pleasant outgoingness and concern. Yet poor Edna was concerned.

"Are you all right?" she said.

Blanch's eyes smiled, a rather hard smile, yet her lips were tender.

"Yes," she said to Edna.

Edna turned, walked slowly to the steps and down. She must have come up rather quickly. Which said something for her. Grade of "D" plus? In overt relationships.

Blanch glanced bitterly at the tiny TV set. Some spy thing was still lumbering on. Perhaps that was it. They were wearing tuxes. The tux doubtless made her think of Paxton. She hoped it was a dream. Because now Paxton, now the spirits of the big house, had left it, had followed her. Come to think of it, she'd seen Paxton in Manhattan too. But that was obviously an optical illusion. And what was to stop one traveling with

Paxton? King Paxton. Companion Paxton.

The sky had been washed by the rains. The stars were brittle, clear. Blanch looked to the bureau. The crystal star. Should she destroy it? Have it sold in one of the numerous antique-curio shops on the Cape? But she felt that she couldn't or wouldn't. She thought sadly of the photos and daguerreotypes of once beloved spouses and relatives that were sold in their gilt frames in the curio shops throughout New England. But the frames had no value once the proud living pictures of people long dead were removed. Using them again almost seemed like re-using a coffin.

What a thought!

She dressed warmly, took the Dart, drove to Lighthouse Beach, left the car on the high, collapsing, paved parking lot, and from behind the fence surveyed the sea ten stories below, the pale quiet breakers. She descended the steep ladder that had not been smashed by the annual storms, descended the hundred feet to the beach, walked over the crusty wet sand, walked beside the sea.

Far far ahead in the surprisingly bright light of this evening she could perceive the end of the bluff, or rather the wall that veered sharply to the west. The ocean seemed to sob and scramble beside her. She removed her shoes and socks, pocketed the latter, laced the shoes together to the top buttonhole of her windbreaker.

The water was warm, certainly warmer than the air. She found herself walking in farther and farther. An ankle, the bottom of her calf. The water tugging at her steadily. It was colder, each inch farther in that she went. She advanced until it was over her calves. They were cold, but she got used to it. She raised her skirt, descended the incline until the water was over her knees. She vowed to flee the first sign of each seventh (Or was it ninth?) wave that would wet her, escaped several times, managed to get her skirt soaked, was sorry that she didn't have a swimsuit on so that she might really immerse herself. She looked up and down the beach. This was really absurd and fun. She could strip and swim. But then she would be wet and cold, and who does that sort of thing?

And then she was glad she hadn't. Someone else was walking along beside her. It is one of the pleasures of the Cape, though, that she wasn't afraid in her loneliness, or in her proximity to this stranger. At least on the central Cape. Lovers of beaches, lovers of the sea, that was all one met at this time of the year. They, and nothing else but this great theater of ocean, narrow beach and high bluff.

There was something about the sea. It said nothing to her but always kept her attention, with its solid portly dignified emptiness. She continued on, with the water over her knees. She hated to leave. The water was thrilling, first cold then warm then cold then warm, her legs alive, burning, charged, yet somewhat numbed. And always the tug at her calves, at her ankles.

The tall figure on the beach stopped, some distance from her. Was it beckoning? No, that could only be imagination. *Hope he isn't waiting for me to try suicide.*

And then she felt she couldn't keep walking on with someone standing there. She returned at an obtuse angle, away from him to the shore, walked farther. Only now her legs felt feverish, the water clammy. The thrill was gone.

She started back, at a tangent that avoided him, she hurried toward the steps. So typical of the Cape, other cars had pulled up above, people stood on the bluff. The warm, comfortable, the safe Cape.

She climbed the steps, at the top she looked down at where she had been. It was miniaturized now, too separated. Not part of her. There was no one on the beach. She opened the door, sat on the car seat with her legs out, brushed the sand from her feet, donned her shoes and socks, started driving back.

What a healthy wholesome trip this had been. No worries. No invasions. She looked down at the spindly little steering wheel, through the mirror saw that she had left the top of the rumble seat open. This was absurd. Of course it was absurd. It wasn't a Model A she was driving. There was no rumble seat. She was in a Dart. What did they call it, one of the bigger "compacts?"

Was she also becoming a repository of antique automobiles?

She sped into Orleans, had a cup of coffee at the Howard Johnson, then a second cup. It would ruin her sleep. But she was not so sure that she wanted to go to sleep, especially after the incident before the TV set.

Next day was bright. With an air of expectancy. Blanch found it almost hard to believe her sensations of the past day. But it had always been that way. Whatever had happened she couldn't quite believe had happened. Was it that they didn't fit into her picture of what life should be? And yet she wondered, what should it be?

But now only the feeling of health filled her. She strode vigorously to the old house. It too seemed open and healthy. She plopped down at her desk, no need for light today. And just as well. The gooseneck lamp that Mallkin had lent her was gone. Perhaps she was supposed to request it each time she needed it.

> some recent actual occurrences have a very suggestive bearing upon the relative degree of immunity from violent and disastrous explosions possessed by the water-tube and

As she was leaving for lunch she encountered Mallkin standing in the driveway.

"Lovely cheery gay day, isn't it?" he said.

"I almost feel like knocking off for the afternoon."

His face fell.

"But I won't," she said.

He seemed happier.

"This is invigorating, this presence of the sea, isn't it?" he said.

"I rather like it. And there's no smog."

"That is an element one must consider. No smog. Indeed one must consider that. Now that you mention it, I have less bronchitic troubles than I had in my Gothamite pre-existence."

Now that she could see it, Mallkin seemed happier than he appeared to be in the past.

has been formed, a further addition of heat increases the temperature again at a much faster ratio to the quantity of heat added,

"Miss Stowe! Miss Stowe!"
She typed on.

much more heat we may apply, the water, as water, at that pressure, cannot be heated any hotter, but changes on the addition of heat to steam; and it is not until we have

"Dear Miss Stowe! Oh, dear Miss Stowe!"
The rain. Never had she seen such rain. This wasn't rain. This was solid water. Great wide flat sheaths smashing across the sea and toward them, hitting the deck, smashing against the bridge, smashing against the large, luxurious windows of their private cabin suite, inundating the ship. There was screaming, especially from the Orientals in the steerage, the jolting shifting of cargo, and then the awful listing of the ship.

"The filthy beasts!" someone shrieked in the companionway. "The filthy beasts! Caulked with cement! See it! Cement! The filthy beasts!"

Benjamin—"No!" she screamed. Then didn't

scream, it wasn't Paxton. Benjamin, tall, haggard Benjamin, rich in his tan, rich in his strong angular face. But now tense, silent, the water smashing about, bells ringing.

"Are they lowering the boats?"

"Miss Stowe! Miss Stowe!"

Mrs.!

Blanch stopped typing. She couldn't recover the frozen image of herself. Or was it herself? Taller. Herself. Benjamin. The cabin. The motion had stopped. The water had frozen midflight, the image collapsed at the edges, melted at the edges, ran down. The conservatory.

Mr. Mallkin standing before her with concern.

"I'm sorry," Blanch said.

"Forgive me . . . My, how totally you dedicate yourself to your typing."

"Has it been long?"

He avoided the question, said, "Miss Stowe, you must be starving. It's evening."

It was almost evening. It had gotten quite dark. The desk lamp was on.

"Blast Paxton," she said, rising.

"I beg your pardon?"

"I'm sorry. Nothing. Had you been in here earlier?"

"Yes. But I didn't want to disturb you. My, you've done a lot of typing."

"Yes," said Blanch. "Yes."

Abstracted, she passed him. It hadn't rained at all. The grass was a bit moist from yesterday, and was beginning to get moistened with the night. It hadn't rained at all.

She felt shattered, shuddered to the sudden image of the mass of water, the thousand drops of boiling white surging into (Do they call them doors on ships?) and through the shattered windows. A body floating and bounding on the water, two bodies. No, three. Who was the third? This was not the first time that she'd had awful thoughts of the water that had taken her parents. She was especially pensive at supper.

Edna hesitantly entered the kitchen, Blanch laughing inside weakly, feeling that if she had dared, Edna would have knocked on the kitchen door. Edna took a little plate of radishes from the refrigerator, selected two, returned the rest; put the two on another dish that she would take to her room.

As she started through the door Blanch said, "When mother and dad were drowned, was there a sort of scandal?"

Edna looked troubled.

"About the ship," Blanch persisted.

"Yes," said Edna. "Odd you should ask. There was some scandal about the caulking. It was to save money. Apparently the proprietor of the shipyard who did it should have been or was well aware that the ship would be doomed in heavy seas. Nothing ever came of it. That is, the prosecution of the culprit."

She looked curiously at Blanch. Blanch said nothing. Edna, the always sad-faced, left the kitchen.

Bye-bye Benjy, bye-bye Ma.

Blanch felt that she was being impelled toward

some sort of solution. She shuddered at what she had just encountered. Not so much that it was awful, but that it was definite. It was clear, whereas the rest of her odd visions had been fantasy of a sort in their lack of concrete proof. But this was another matter, even though here too there had been a mixing of images, the unclarity of at least her father's face, the confusion of Paxton with her father for a moment.

But at least she now felt that she had actually seen her mother, so elegant with her honest, deepset eyes, firm classic nose but for a whimsical slight uptilt, and strong yet passionate mouth, one for command and laughter. She had never really seen her before. The wedding picture had been meaningless. Blanch knew that no person could have looked like that. And there were pictures of Benjamin, her father. But snapshots as a boy, then school photos that seemed false. And then puppets again in the wedding portrait by Bachrach. But she had seen her mother and father this day, they were terribly real, "terribly" in the sense that they who were dead had not died, which somehow seemed to erase the present Blanch Stowe, of Shoreham on Cape Cod—or at least time. For if wet grass, rich grass thick with globes of dew or rain moisture, should suddenly re-exist, what of the dried and dead grass it replaced? Something like that. Yet she wanted to reach toward them. The two in white clothes. Inundated in white foam. Sucked into a white whorl of sea. Murdered most foul.

Maddest of all, she felt that she was Benjamin

as well as the woman her mother, at the very moment when she was observing both of them. And that wasn't too mad a concept—it could be argued that each parent contributed their blood. Yet there seemed more than that. It seemed as though Benjamin were her mother and her mother were Benjamin, which was obviously absurd, Blanch could only conclude. How madly she was jumbling things up in her mind and memory. And of course her mother's name had been Blanch too. What a mix-up!

NEITHER weather, light nor Cape could cheer her as she went to work next day. Would there be further revelations? Why couldn't she quit? But she had quit, she had gone to New York. Actually she felt a little poignant satisfaction that she was not the worse for yesterday. The drowning of her parents which she had witnessed had been horrible, but something had been clear—if only it was the appearance of two people whom she had never knowingly conjured, or experienced the sensation of having seen alive in the past. Her parents had come home to her. Had come home to leave, but she had seen them.

The typewriter, the lamp were like the *(Is there a word for it?)* the thing that sets the willing hypnotic subject off. She began to type

marked "gold" and "steel" show the relation

to heat and temperature and the melting points of these metals. All the inclined

BLANCH! BLANCH! BLANCH! BLANCH! BLANCH! BLANCH!

She was Blanch. The mother was Blanch. The daughter was Blanch. The daughter was Blanch. The mother was Blanch.

They were furious.

The woman who had drowned, younger, equine, lovely and horsy, bristling with fury. The mother staid, her face hardened by contest.

"You're mad to—" said the mother.

"Why? Tell me why. He's the right sort, been to the best schools—"

"He has nothing."

"Our family wasn't always wealthy."

"There's more to it than that."

"What?"

"I don't care to say."

"I know why you don't 'care to say,'" said the daughter.

The mother turned on her furiously. "There's no call for that."

"You don't care to say because you don't know."

The mother turned away. Grimly, "One doesn't have to 'know.'"

"Oh my! Blood! Call of race!"

"You needn't be so insolent."

The daughter's lips quivered.

But it was wrong, it was all wrong. She'd had

this happen on the Cape and it wasn't on the Cape. Brown and grey stone houses. They had just come back from—does Meadowbrook make sense? It didn't to Blanch. And the clothes were wrong. For a moment it had been the tight hairdo's of the thirties, as though they wore shellacked wigs. And this was crazy, because it wasn't until after the war that her parents had met. The time element was all mixed up.

And then—this was unbelievable—Blanch was in a kitchen that cried bleak poverty—or her awareness was. A child was sitting at the table, and Blanch could recognize the child as Edna, some seventy years younger. The child Edna was saying, "Why don't I have a daddy?" and the mother, with that same pained look Edna wore so frequently (and that Aaron did too!) was both saying yet not saying (or she had said this or hinted it through the years, there was some sort of "sign" statement here): "Your father has decided that this was not to be, and now is gone from us." "Is he dead?" said Edna/Aaron, for now the tot's face was, or may have been, either the young Edna or Aaron, they would look so much alike when they were old, as old couples do, and it was hard now to keep a steady image of anything. "It would be easier to consider him so," said Aaron/Edna's mother. "Do we hate him, Mummy?" "No. That we are not permitted, nor need we love."

It may have been said at one time.

MILAN GAZED at her hesitantly from the door. Blanch smiled, asked him in. Holding an open book, Aaron sat in his corner. Edna was in her room.

"I'll be right with you."

Blanch got her things. They drove off in Milan's car.

"Whither, whither?"

"I'd like to take you to a really big spread."

"You're out of luck, I've eaten."

"But I haven't."

"I'll watch you. What's up?"

"I couldn't believe it, They're paying an absurd amount for one of my paintings."

"How wonderful!"

"Limitations. It's going to be used in a pharmaceutical ad."

"Well—at least you'll be reproduced."

"Oh I keep the rights to the picture, I insisted on that. It's unusual and they thought I was insane. But I told them, 'Make up your mind. If you want to hang it in some executive's home or office, you'll buy the painting. If you want to use it for an ad, you'll buy the rights. If you want to use it for both you'll have to pay for both. Plus a contract for a percentage each time it's sold again.' "

"How did they react?"

"They ripped. They went crazy. But I think they liked it, too. The straight mercenariness of it."

"So where are we going?"

At dinner Milan unembarrassedly gorged himself, and Blanch found herself able to eat another meal, though not as gluttonish a one as Milan's.

At the end, when Milan was rosy with expensive wine and rich food, he looked at Blanch and said, "Nice time to say it, but I'm scared."

She knew for whom he was worried, but she felt strangely uninvolved. There seemed to be so many Blanches, the Blanch—or Blanches—of the big house, one with bare and powdered shoulders and bodice of olive velvet, graceful and sharp as a spray shot from a hose, others with tasseled flapper hemlines or Victorian bustles, Blanches in the bleak sacks of World War One and the gleaming white of turn-of-the-century boating outfits, and this casually clad Blanch of Milan and the restaurant—so many Blanches that she felt she could be objective, even if a bit selfish.

But she remembered what she had encountered recently, said, "In a way, things are better. And I've become systematic."

He looked at her curiously. "Systematic about what? Spooks?"

"Maybe. I'm beginning to single people out. I mean, before, by costume and that sort of thing, I guessed which one might have been a grandmother, maybe even a great-grandmother. But today I," she hesitated in saying this, it did sound crazy, "I met two, no four different people."

Milan waited.

"I was in at the death of my mother and father." She disregarded, though was thankful for, Milan's pained look. "I overheard something." She told him about the caulking. "There's no reason I should have known about that," she said.

"Unless you overheard it as a child."

"And they looked so elegant and rich!" Blanch remembered. Then, "I think that's possible but I don't see why that should come now. And frankly, I don't think I've ever heard much of anything discussed by Edna and Aaron."

"Freud says you never forget."

"The others—" She told of the conversation between tiny Edna and her mother. And wondered if it had been Edna.

Milan's distress continued. "I mean it. It's like establishing— But let's say you have extra-sensory perception. I don't see how you're going to wind up living in a world with not only real people but also all the people who are dead."

"Come to think of it," Blanch said, "there haven't been many people in my world."

"That's what gets me," said Milan. "If you don't feel what I'm trying to say is an insult— you're so normal. In spite of your childhood."

Blanch laughed. "Well, do you want me to flip?"

"No. I guess that's just New England that makes me feel it's unusual for anybody to be normal."

"You're New England too," she chided.

"We're first generation," he said defensively.

"Big deal."

"I was just wondering. About you and the type-writer," Milan mused. "The way it sets you going. I wonder—"

"What?" said Blanch.

"No. It's crazy."

"No. Really."

"I'll have to—"

Her eyes told him that either he had to tell her, or shouldn't have begun.

"If the typing sets you off in the way it does, in the big house—"

"Yes?"

"What if you did some of this hypnotic typing or whatever it is, elsewhere?"

"I could."

"I mean, things have been happening to you in the big house. Now if things from elsewhere came to you as you're typing in the big house, might not things at the big house that you're not aware of come to you—well, elsewhere?"

"I think I get you, and I think you've got an interesting point."

"Because there are things peculiar to the big house."

"Like Hugh, and the party."

"I don't know, though," Milan groaned. "I don't like the whole business. I think we're fooling around too much."

"Look," Blanch said, "since things have happened, I think either we're going to face it frankly— Oops!" She put her hand to her mouth. "There I go, bossy me, saying we again—"

"You better say we," Milan insisted. "I'm up to my ears in it now."

"So let's face it out. Instead of having it—irk. Or fester."

Milan, with a bleak expression, confessed, "You don't know what this is doing to me."

Blanch blushed, her eyes moistened. She touched his hand.

He sort of shuffled in his chair, said, "Let's see what the off-season discotheques are like."

Later, as he let her out at her home, Blanch said, "Tomorrow night I type!"

"But what about work? Oh, you don't work Saturdays anyway."

"No."

Milan looked worried as he said good-bye and drove off.

THE NEXT night Blanch appeared in the Dart with paper and typewriter. Milan rushed down the steps. He took the portable from her hand. The gesture made her feel silly, the machine was absurdly light, but it was so like Milan. He opened the door for her.

He had arranged what was no more than a wooden end table, a floor lamp beside it, and a kitchen chair.

"This is it," he said, "but why don't you first rest a bit?"

Blanch sat down on the rickety divan, laughed. She was excited and a bit frightened.

Milan rushed into the next room, came back with a book, which he had obviously grabbed at random, placed it on the table.

"How silly. I didn't think of bringing copy," she said. Then, "Actually there's nothing stopping us."

Milan looked at her a bit helplessly, shrugged. She removed her jacket and sat down at the typewriter.

"What are you going to do?" she asked Milan.

"I guess I might as well go to work."

"But what about your projecting?"

"I've set it up in the kitchen. I'm just going to do some retouching. Reworking, anyway."

"Tallyho," said Blanch.

Milan looked worried, shrugged, presumably for encouragement, and left the room.

Blanch looked about her. There probably wasn't a thing in the cottage that belonged to Milan. And yet this was all Milan. Because even as a camp is sparse, and yet ready for life, for fun, this was Milan, decks cleared for action, as it were. No impediments.

She began to type from the book he had brought her.

I should not venture to speak thus strongly if my justification were not to be found in the simplest and most obvious of facts—if it

needed more than an appeal to the most no-
torious truths to justify my assertion, that
the improvement of

and so on.

Gradually, then forcefully, she felt a drawing
away as though someone had hooked, not into
her viscera, but as though someone had drawn a
set of diminishing circles over the area she occupied, and that the central circle was an area from
which all energy was being drained, all light
blotted out.

thus far, it is irrational to doubt that he went
further to find, as we do, that upon that brief
gladness there follows a certain

She was walking the halls of the big house. She
seemed to be walking them endlessly, patroling
them, the servants' quarters, the lower quarters.
There were people about. Hugh was screaming.
The chiropractor had strapped him to the bench.
Rather, tied his wrists down, with the fastenings
going under the bench. The legs were tied down,
too. The wailing was incredible. That, and
Hugh's popping eyes and sweat.

The homeopath was saying to Mr. Mallkin,
"This is it. This is the only way. You have no
right to interfere. Stick to the agreement."

And Mr. Mallkin saying, "I can't be responsible. I'll not be responsible," and running into the
hall and saying, "Oh my God! Oh my God! This
is terrible. Oh my God! What will become of

all of us?" and the homeopath yelling after him, "There can only be one captain to this ship." And Mr. Mallkin pressing his hands to his ears and running off. And Blanch patroling.

She'd never been to Mr. Mallkin's room, and yet she knew that this was his room. Stuffed cretonne easy chair, glass-shelved bookcases jammed with books, ill chosen and probably picked up cheaply and in bulk. Heavy, scratched, probably Salvation Army thrift store furniture. That hideous lamp on his long table, with its silk shade and dusty tassels. And his brass bed, ugly and expensive. An heirloom? His clothes hung on a small rack with a cotton curtain hanging before it.

Now Mr. Mallkin was sitting in his stuffed chair. A man, who could have been any one of the men the night of the party, sat on the bed. Another man sat in a straight chair near a little round table with some writing materials on it. The man on the bed sportily dressed, in his forties, with thinning hair and sleek face-flesh.

"It's not as though we're renting something from a total stranger."

Mr. Mallkin said, "That's not it at all. I have terrible expenses."

The one at the table asked, "Really?"

"You don't understand," Mallkin said. "To justify my having this, it has to be run as a business. And if I'm going to run it as a business, you'll have to pay a realistic rent."

"But it's going to be a loss, you said so yourself."

"Yes. But Internal Revenue will not consider

it seriously unless this rental appears valid. Now I know that I can pretend I received more than you paid me. But they discover things like that."

And the man at the table saying, "It's not that we can't do it. And it's not, as you know, that we're not going to do it. But really!"

Blanch walking the floors.

But was she Blanch, in her tiny, shiny black shoes with straps across the arches, black stockings, the rich black dress? As she climbed the last step to the servants' landing, powerful arms with iron biceps caught her, crushed her against the male toughness of a body beneath female garments. She gasped, screamed into the dark, a long coiling shriek, almost as quickly regretted it, tried to wallow up out of it, to Milan's lunging into the room, leaning over and embracing her from behind, nuzzling her cheek and burying his face in her hair, saying, "Blanch, darling, you poor kid, Blanch!"

Shaken at this tenderness she'd never known, wanting it tremendously, yet at the same time, being a Stowe or whatever it was, firmly though gently, she said, "Milan, Milan, forgive me." Now almost completely recovered though still shaken, she said as perhaps a young Edna would have said, "That was the silliest thing!" in harsh self-judgment.

Milan stamped off in impatience and despair, gave his thigh a resounding slap, turned and with loving reproof said, "The things you do to hide your—" *Gentleness, softness, loveliness?* What could he say, all true, to reach her? The poor pushed-around kid.

He sighed, shook his head, said simply, "Blanch, you must know what you mean to me," and then stopped in his inarticulateness.

But he didn't have to say more, could see on her gentle troubled features that she understood. He could sense her eager thanks for what was little more than a hope of happiness, though her being Blanch made it a despairing one at that. Without a word she conveyed that she wanted terribly what he offered, perhaps joyously. But because she was Blanch? a Stowe? or because of the chimera or real evil that beset her?—they could not begin to really try so long as the puzzle was not solved one way or the other.

There was no time for the luxury of tender thoughts.

He slumped on the battered wicker sofa, looked at her and said, "Okay?"

"Yes."

But she blushed and whipped her head away.

Milan was shaken by the fullness in his heart. More to stop her embarrassment than get started, he said, "Okay, what was it this time?"

Blanch found herself tightening, reluctant to speak. She winced, smiled sadly at her resistance, then said, "I was on the servants' landing. I—" She laughed a bit hysterically. "I'm afraid I was captured. Embraced by these two great big arms. Not Mallkin's!" She had to laugh at this. "I was wearing an old costume—"

She looked confused.

"Yes?"

"It didn't seem like a woman!"

"What do you mean?"

"But why the dress?" she wondered aloud.

Milan waited.

"I don't know," she worried. "And earlier, I was walking on the second floor. I had on these tight, strapped black shoes. I don't know what decade—or century—that was. After I got away from those powerful arms, I don't know how I got the chance or light to see but—I had button shoes!"

"Did anything else happen?"

"As a matter of fact, yes."

She told of Hugh strapped to the bench and going it cold turkey, the argument between the osteopath and Mr. Mallkin, and of Mr. Mallkin arranging for the house rental, presumably for the party.

Strange. Total recall of the non-encountered.

"Oh! This is the silliest and most hideous of things."

"What?"

"When they were discussing the rental, one fellow sat on a chair, Mallkin sat on a chair, another fellow sat on the bed. The one who was sitting on the bed, now I can see it! Unbeknownst to the other two had a small—no, it was a single-edge razor blade!—that must have been it—and he was slashing the coverlet, and I swear he was slashing into the mattress."

"That's disgusting," said Milan. Then, "I

hope these aren't your fantasies." More as a joke.

"Isn't it? Such a hideous, childish creature. I always wondered who slashed seats in theaters."

Now she seemed relaxed and good humored, for which Milan both marveled and was thankful.

"I think we ought to knock off," he suggested.

"But it was just getting interesting."

Milan looked irked. "Yes, but what of the last thing that happened—?"

She looked at him questioningly.

"The thing that made you scream."

"But it didn't happen to me," Blanch said.

Milan said, "I don't care." His voice shook with concern as he suggested, "Have you ever thought, what if you don't come back?"

Blanch gasped. But almost as quickly her eyes flashed, fighting the concept.

She softened as she studied Milan's sympathetic pain, said, "Just a little more. Please. I really think I'm in control."

"I don't," he persisted.

She looked at him sadly, then played her trump card.

"And what if it's more serious if I stop than if I go on?"

He paled, looked at her for some time.

Then he glared at the typewriter, arose and left the room.

though the superstructure remained for long

ages so slight and feeble as to be compatible
with the existence of almost any general

Still in black. In black? The gaiety of the
clothes of the others.

She was going to the south outbuilding. She
felt very strong. And very grim. She could hear
children calling from the Bay side of the house.

She entered, it was a stable. A lovely pony stood
there. Coal black. Black Beauty with a star on
its forehead. Great trusting eyes. She petted it,
forced it down until it was lying, strange, lying,
turned its head slowly, deftly but fiercely slashed
its throat with a butcher knife. There was much
to cut. Its eyes went wild, it struggled desperately, she (he?) had her knee on one of its shoulders,
keeping it down, its blood squirting, it was
neighing pitiably, horrible air sounds coming
from its neck.

She wasn't running. The lawn, the garden were
jaunting, were shaking before heavy masculine
steps, before a moving consciousness, that entered
the big house.

"This has to stop!" Milan was saying, "This has
to stop!"

Blanch found her forehead soaked with per-
spiration. Milan was holding her wrist with both
hands.

"Blanch, this has to stop! This has to stop!
What happened?"

Blanch said, "I don't know what happened."

"You were sick, you were—I don't know!"

"I'll type some more," Blanch said.

"That's all for tonight."

"I'll type some more."

Not unkindly, Milan raised her to her feet by her wrists, led her to the divan, sat her down and hurried to the kitchen. He returned with a bottle of wine and a glass, looking sheepish.

"No. Coffee."

He rushed out, returned almost immediately. "It's heating. If you saw yourself—"

"Was I typing?"

"No. You'd stopped. I mean, you were typing, and then you stopped. You kept looking at the page as though you were reading. But there was a terrible expression on your face. No, it wasn't your face! It wasn't you. I never saw anything like it."

"This old medium idea wasn't so cockeyed."

He shrugged, then asked, "What happened?"

Blanch was on the verge of saying a tactful Nothing, but knew that she could not lie. That was something a Stowe never did, never thought of doing. She could refuse to talk but she wouldn't lie.

"Look at your hand," he said.

It was clenched, as though she were still holding the knife. She opened it, stretched it hard and wide, rested it on her thigh.

The water was boiling.

Milan went to the kitchen and came back with two cups of coffee.

"That's enough of it," he said with finality.

"We've had our games for the night."

Blanch said nothing. Milan returned to the kitchen, brought Ritz crackers and cottage cheese. Blanch found herself hungry, Milan must have too. They ate wildly, refilled their cups in the kitchen.

"Okay," Milan said. He seemed to have recovered, though he seemed to have had more of a shock than she. "Let's have it."

"The second part," she said.

"Yes. The second part."

"I found myself slashing a throat—jugular vein—of a lovely pony. I?!"

"Charming! Just an isolated image? Or were there surroundings?"

"Oh no. It was the south outbuilding. I—it—whatever it was—entered the building with that one purpose—"

"What do you mean by 'whatever it was'?"

"It was dressed like a woman."

"Was it a man?"

"I don't know." She continued, " 'It' got the pony to lie down. Whoever was doing it was very strong. The pony really went mad at the slashing. But 'it' had its knee right into its shoulder and kept it down. It must have taken absolutely fantastic strength."

"Then what?"

"That was it."

"Anyone else around?"

"There were children's voices on the other side of the big house, on the beach side."

"That's really cute. Having read my share of gothic novels, I'm a little worried."

"Possession?" Blanch said.

"Yes."

"I don't believe that at all, though. You don't either."

"Well . . ." he said.

"You've got to admit that this is awfully interesting."

Somehow they both seemed gayer after this experiment. At his place it was almost a parlor game, a thing to be treasured because it was exciting. Something, too, that they might eventually lose.

They parted that night with no agreement about whether they would resume the experiment. Casually, Milan rested his hands lightly on her shoulders, and Blanch smiled up at him. Neither spoke, but both knew that theirs had become a newer, closer relationship.

She ran up to her bedroom hoping, *"Oh God, oh God, I hope that this time this is it, that it won't change, that it won't get crumbed up, that it isn't just one of those so many things."*

BLANCH SPENT a fitful night. For the first time she felt that she had encountered something malevolent from within. Not as her childhood fear of Paxton, nor the assault on the upper steps. But since the cutting of the pony's throat she felt that she had been within a being who had done something awful.

Next morning for the first time she felt afraid to go to work, hoped that whatever transmission she encountered would not be actively evil.

She entered the big house to find Mallkin jauntily strutting about in the main hall. He said good morning to her, his eyes twinkling as he waved a letter. Not at her, but he was waving a letter. He seemed extremely cheery, a condition that communicated itself to Blanch.

"Good morning," she said, with a richness that surprised her.

He stopped, suddenly seemed shy, apologetic, ingratiating. Then his eyes became flat.

"Yes," he said, "Yes. Good morning," and turned, but she distinctly heard him say something about privacy.

As a matter of fact she had been in his room, a distinct invasion of privacy, the preceding night at Milan's—or rather, one night before the festivities at the big house. In that sense she was guilty, knowingly so. But on the other hand she was a bit frightened too, because whatever privacy he felt was invaded, unless he knowingly participated in her strange vision of the night before, must have been invaded by someone else. And with Hugh, Hugh's new bride, and the osteopath gone, if they were gone, there should only have been Mallkin in the house.

If Mallkin was even in the house at night. For

instance, where did Mallkin eat? This still troubled her. She had seen his room, there was no food in it. Was there another apartment in the place? A gatekeeper's lodge or something of that sort?

It was all so eerie.

She returned to the typewriter. She was so disturbed that for the first time she saw the words before her that she typed, that is, was aware of them. She almost felt that she would welcome one of the mad transmigrations she had been experiencing. Still troubled, she left early for lunch.

But not a woman to delay, to let subtlety become cowardice, she stopped in the main hall, looked up and called loudly, "Mr. Mallkin! Mr. Mallkin!"

There was silence. She waited. And then again called, very loudly, "Mr. Mallkin!" a bit distressed at the harshness and demand in her voice.

She heard his door open. She could hardly hear him. He was barefoot or in carpet slippers. He came to the balcony and looked down. It seemed to be the old Mallkin. But she had to finish what she had set out to do.

"This morning you mentioned something about privacy. Have I disturbed you in any way?"

"Privacy? Privacy?"

"Yes, Mr. Mallkin. I don't want to be pushy. But you did say it and I'm really distressed if you feel that I've somehow invaded—I've only seen you in the halls."

She felt a pang of guilt. Their running about at night and looking into rooms when they'd been drawn into the party wasn't that innocent. But she'd gone as far as she dared.

Mr. Mallkin looked at her long and silently, and then said, "Miss Stowe, will you be so kind as to wait for a moment."

She heard him toddle off, come back heavier on his shoes, tiny loafers for so immense a man, clattering down the stairs.

"I'm glad you caught me up on that. I don't believe people should have secrets. Do you?"

Blanch said nothing. It was a tricky question.

"I don't lock the place," Mr. Mallkin said. "I didn't lock the place when I drove into town this morning." (So he had a car.) "When I returned, I distinctly knew that someone had been in my room. Things had been moved about. It was only that papers had been moved inches. But I am a meticulous individual and I know. I now realize that I was taking my pet out on an innocent person, that you had come for the first time this morning. I beg that you appreciate my distress."

Blanch didn't know what to say, said, "I envy your courage in being able to stay alone in so big a place."

Mr. Mallkin said, with a lush satisfaction, "I am not alone. I commune."

This was his offhand, sneakily added equivalent of his earlier "privacy" remark. He was not a pleasant person. Anything to confuse one.

Blanch went home to lunch. Edna had picked

up a letter from Gloria at the post office. Blanch felt guilty as she opened it. All that food.

She paled as she read it.

The trip had been fine. Gloria had met "some real dopes and some real dolls." And then, misfortune. When she returned she found "the apartment had been attacked with a knife. Mattresses, furniture, cushions, paintings, window shades and drapes *slashed!* Oh, carpets and rugs too." Of course the insurance covered it, even to having the paintings restored. But how awful! "If you or I had been there during such a maniac's onslaught!"

Blanch thought she was going to faint and sat down. No questioning look from Edna this time, who was standing before her with a glass of water.

Edna didn't ask, Blanch didn't tell her. For Edna would always have that agonized, questioning look. And Edna didn't know Gloria, anyway.

Absurd! Such a series of coincidences. And the pony was slashed such a very long time ago. Still, Mallkin's distress. Though when the apartment was vandalized Blanch was nowhere near New York. "Nothing stolen." Slashed and ripped. Hideous coincidences.

SHE DECIDED not to go to work that afternoon. She'd had enough. Nor would she drive, she needed to walk. She briskly walked the mile and a half to Milan's place.

He must have worked or worried all night. He was lumbering around, he had just gotten up ("and sleepless lovers wake at noon"). At her knock he had at least put on his pants. He was still wearing his pajama top.

"Coffee," he mumbled. "Breakfast? Lunch?"

"You finish up," Blanch said. "I'm going to make brunch for both of us."

She poached eggs, fried bacon, made toast and coffee as Milan bathed and shaved.

He looked fresh, eager, when he sat down, and then drooped at the expression on her face.

"What's the spook news today?" he said.

He was not flippant. He was angry. At his competition.

Blanch told him of the letter. She repeated and he concurred with her conclusion that it could only be coincidence.

But then, looking angrier than before, because he knew that he was speaking sense, he added, "But I do feel that this sort of fooling around you're doing produces such coincidences. I mean, you live on a reasonable level of—you know—"

"Dullness" was the word he didn't want to say. But wasn't it the truth?

"Once you get into this area, these coincidences are more likely to happen—I think. I mean, maybe there are no such things as coincidences, but tendencies *toward*."

She told him about Mallkin's disturbed papers.

"This is weird," he gloomed. "I mean, we're having a time. Me vicariously, you actually. Where do we go from here? Although I do wish you'd never go near that house again."

"It's too late," she said, remembering her drowsing before the TV set, when Paxton had penetrated her very bedroom.

BLANCH WOKE shortly after dawn. She could feel that it would be one of those running days—in which the tide, the waves, ran before the wind, and the trees rustled.

By the time that she had dressed and eaten, the sky had greyed, was leaden. But there was vigor in the air. She almost sprinted down to the Bay. The tide was high.

She walked beside it, south. There was no one in sight.

She looked at the restless water and thought about the multitudinous lives of things that lived beneath it, and she could not help but think of the multitudinous life ashore, and of human lives that had preceded her.

Other than these philosophical or metaphysical, or merely melancholy, thoughts, Blanch was not particularly affected. She walked on, beyond stretches not yet bought-up or built on, past other homes along the Bay, forests, forest roads, until at last she started back, vibrant, her mind alive, yet with no definable thinking, merely a sense of health.

Suddenly she felt weak, as though she would pass out. She looked desperately about. Where was the big house? There was no big house. Just scrub pines and sand.

She felt bruised. There was sand all over her great black skirt. She felt torn about inside, found herself staggering in pain and weakness. She more felt than saw the hideous yokel, tall and drably clad, disappearing into the trees.

She gasped in agony, fell to her knees. This was ruin indeed. She vomited, forced herself to fall away from it, onto the sand, lay weeping.

Could her shame ever be concealed? If only she could have him apprehended, punished. But she dared not, could not. All she could do was hope that he would go out of her life. That nothing would result.

She was weeping madly, her loosened hair over her face moistened by tears, messy with sand.

And then she did not weep.

Looking at the sand, playing with the sand.

Smooth young fingers playing with the sand.

This was such fun, lying in the sand. She knew they should, could, see her from the great house. It would be just like Paxton to see her. And to see that she were punished for lying in the sand, trust him for that. She sat up, took a sea shell and rested it in the lap of her bright starchy pinafore. Let them get angry. The sun was bright. Yet awful. Only it wasn't she and the pinafore. She stood on the beach. She who had wept. Nothing to weep for now.

The young man came up, humbly holding his hat. She looked deeply into his eyes. She knew immediately, instinctively that there was something familiar, something recognizable, of someone she had not fully seen. There was pride and of course love, how could one escape it? The tall, erect, hard-faced dark and steely-eyed man of twenty-two, half her age, modestly, correctly dressed, holding his bowler in his hands. No, he had a walleye. But a fine figure of a man.

"So you've been in service."

"Aye, Madam."

She fingered the cameo brooch on the bodice of her black dress, said, "Your characters do you well."

"Thank you Madam."

"Despite your age, you will be head butler."

Paxton's face hardened. That was all. The wall-eye helped maintain separation, would properly cow the maids.

Perversely, "Tell me of your parents."

"I was orphaned, Madam."

"Who reared you?"

"Distant kin, Madam."

And that's how it would always be. He would never know. A fine, strong man. How much he resembled herself at that age. But without the key he—no one—would ever know.

A fine woman. I know how far I may go and how far I may not go. But I shall rule this house.

And not the proper Mr. Pierson.

He looked steadily at the woman before him. With his good eye, that is. He knew things that cannot be verbalized. They would live together, work together, bolster each other without invading each other's domain.

I am Blanch and do not like you. Great hulking cruel bossy dark-eyed man. King of the Great House, with your frightening walleye. Deferential always, especially to mama. But king. Tyrant. Julius Caesar. You can threaten me and you can clutch me. Daddy never does. But Paxton, some day I'll split your head. Some day I'll split your head, Paxton.

Blanch found herself walking down to the water. Automobiles honked from the other side of the house, their occupants wanting her to run off with them, at least to exchange parting words. She looked at her pumps and silk stockings, their whiteness giving more shape to her legs, so much of them visible below her tasseled flapper hem. They seemed so idiotic on the beach. The beach was a place for bathing suits and running in the sun. Yet her dress seemed of the beach. The colors were all so right—white, yellow, the bars of yellow and brown. How could they have worn the silly dark colors of mummy's time, grandmummy's time?

Edna watched this elegantly dressed woman near the shoreline. Edna stood far off, in the pines, holding the little guidebook, *Shore and Deep*. She was looking for sea shells, identifying them. And there the elegant Miss Inscho in her gay clothes. What sort of wasted life was it, that those people led? They seemed so gay. But what did they do for others? for the poor and halt?

Aaron came up. Edna turned. It wasn't Aaron, it was Milan.

Simply, Blanch said, "I've been all over, in time. Generations. Up and back. Family to family. In minutes."

Milan seemed concerned but not as worried as before.

"It doesn't seem to have hit you too much this time."

"I think things are clearing up."

They strolled beside the water.

"You're up early."

"I guess," Blanch said, "I could say that I was 'called.' On these exciting running days, I just have to get out. And then I encountered all sorts of people."

Milan waited.

"I'm going to have to sort them out. It was really amazing. Different names. I can check on those. In fact I know them. Inscho. Pierson."

"Who was Pierson?"

"That was great-great-grandmother. And Inscho —my great-grandmother married Inscho."

"Well, that follows."

"Yes, but I'm seeing other people. This Paxton. And then—really strange—I was Edna for a bit."

And yet, had she been Edna? That was least clear.

"I thought you'd added her to your collection once before."

When, as a little girl, Edna had been talking to her mother. Milan was right.

They were strolling to the road which led to Blanch's house.

"Great," Milan said, sourly, "so you're straightening things out." Then, "I suppose this may have some scientific merit. Are you keeping an account of it?"

"No. I'm not."

He looked at Blanch curiously.

"If it's an isolated thing, it's my own business," she reasoned. "And if it's not isolated, I'm sure the world will get to know about it. How do we know this isn't happening with a lot of people?"

"I suspect it isn't," Milan said, with a grin.

They let it go at that.

He walked almost to the house before he said, "Well, I'm going to go on with my stroll. It's still early. When do you go to work?"

"Generally nine or ten o'clock."

"Well . . ."

They had both grown to like each other very much. They had merely to look at each other to convey much that was nonverbal. And then parted. He almost at the door.

How many times had she opened this kitchen door? The sound of birds and trees. The sound of the Cape. The sound of water and breeze.

She put the kettle on. She would have another cup of coffee before going to work. She could change her shoes.

She stepped into the hall and gasped.

Edna sat on the floor in the living room, leaning her back weakly against the wall. Blanch rushed to her.

"Darling, what is it? Can you get up? May I help?"

"Please do," said Edna.

Blanch helped her up and led her to a chair.

Edna was silent. Then, "Is that hot water?"

"Yes. Shall I call Dr. Wemyss—"

"I don't think that will be necessary," Edna said, rising with difficulty, Blanch running to help her. "No," Edna said, refusing aid. "I've got to take stock of myself."

She walked slowly about the room.

"What happened?"

"I've been very fortunate," she said. "I don't think I'm injured."

"What did you trip on?"

"I'd like some tea."

Blanch said, "That's enough of this. What happened to you? Did you faint? Was it a stroke?"

There wasn't that curious, agonized look in Edna's expression now.

She turned to Blanch and said, "I was thrown down."

"Someone was here?"

"Yes. A woman."

"Can you describe her? Did you get a good look at her?"

"Barely. She was little more than a flurry in the corner of my eye. One doesn't see much with peripheral vision at my age. A flurry of—"

"Petticoats, long dress?"

"Yes," Edna said.

But I may have planted that in her.

"Who would do such a thing? What happened?"

"It was as though someone had run down the stairs past me and shoved me."

"Aaron?"

"I presume he is in his room. He *is* in his room."

Blanch rushed there. Aaron lay still on his bed. Generally at this hour he was dressed. But now he was dead, his eyes open. A horrible look in his eyes? Or just the look of the dead? Blanch rushed from the room, leaned against the wall.

"May I have some tea?"

"Yes," said Blanch. "Yes."

With shaking hands she made two cups of tea, brought one to Edna.

Edna sipped. "I'm feeling better," she said. "I've been fortunate. Aaron's dead, isn't he?"

Blanch looked at Edna in confusion, said, "Yes. Had you seen?"

"No," said Edna.

"What's the matter with me?" Blanch said. She ran to the phone, called Dr. Wemyss, returned to the living room.

"Terrible things have been happening," Blanch said.

"Terrible things have always been happening," said Edna.

"I mean, experiences that I have been having."

There had been a lambent rationality, a quiet

awareness and bravery, in Edna's last statement. Now that pained look of Edna's returned, that expression that tended to stifle any further talk on Blanch's part. But Blanch persisted.

"How old was Aaron?"

"He was born in 1887," said Edna.

"Then he was much older than you!"

"Thirteen years." And then, with the closest thing to a little smile that Blanch had ever seen on Edna's face, her grandmother said, "When we got married, he was thirteen years older than I. But as you get older, the ratio diminishes."

Blanch felt ill, said, "I think I wish I could cry."

Edna said, "You didn't have much of a life with us. When you were born, I was fifty-two. Fifty-three when you came to stay with us permanently."

"What was Benjamin—what was my father—like?"

"He was like Aaron. He never spoke much. That is, to us. Always in school, on scholarships. And then he worked at summer camps."

"He was like Aaron?"

"Yes. Not the Aaron you knew. For the last twenty years he has not been with us. And yet like Aaron. He was a person of silences. But you see, Aaron's father, whom Aaron didn't know, was said to be a very hard and very strong man. He left—"

Edna looked at Blanch closely.

"Good heavens!" Blanch said. "Then your father—?"

"Yes?"

Then it had not been Edna speaking to her mother. Could it have been Aaron speaking to his mother? Confusion! It was all so confused.

The physician's car pulled into the driveway. Dr. Wemyss entered, self-assured, heavy footed, professional, kind.

He went directly to Edna, took her hand, looked into her eyes. Tears came to Blanch's eyes when she saw the confident friendliness of the old man and woman before her.

Dr. Wemyss went into Aaron's room, came out in a moment.

"Of course Pilchard?"

"Yes," Edna said as quickly.

He phoned the undertaker.

To Edna he said, "I've told Mrs. Wemyss to come over."

Edna said nothing, emanated sweet, grave dignity.

THERE WERE no calling hours, no service, no relatives who had to be informed. It had been the way of their religion and Aaron's own wishes, and presumably would be so, eventually, for Edna. Merely a wet, blowing morning, with Dr. Wemyss, his wife, Edna, Blanch and Milan, who had insisted on coming, in his worn sports jacket, worn dress slacks, and a tattered plastic raincoat that had been mended with bandage tape. Blanch had never liked Milan as much. They all rode in the physician's limousine, followed the hearse to the small graveyard between marsh and field and Bay.

There was no sadness in the interment. A very old man died, in a lovely area, and now was laid to rest in a beautiful field.

Dr. Wemyss tried to prevail on Edna to dine with him and his wife, and of course Blanch and —with a hard, approving glance—Milan. But Edna would have none of it.

Edna, remarkably tranquil, almost easy, on this day indicated to Blanch she wanted to be alone and seemed happy when Blanch said that she and Milan would eat out.

THE MORNING had been as any other morning. Edna at her writing table in her room, or reading in the overstuffed chair beside it. Of Aaron there was no real absence, of one who had so long never been present, at least barely, in Blanch's memory. Had he been senile for the last fifteen or twenty years? Or had that been Aaron at all times? Yet Blanch had to remember that Aaron had lost an only son. It must have been a terrible blow.

Other than Edna sending all of Aaron's clothes to Morgan Memorial's Goodwill Charities, there had been no change in his possessions. His room was as it had been, lacking only him and his clothes. The house had been spacious for three people, as so many New England houses are.

Aaron had died on a Friday. Blanch did not return to work until Tuesday. She had hardly sat down to type when Mr. Mallkin came in.

He said, "How awful of me, I've just learned of your father's death—"

"Grandfather," said Blanch.

"Oh. Well, I am so sorry. I would like to have done something."

"There was nothing you could have done," Blanch said sincerely.

"It does make one feel guilty. But then, I've had such trouble here in the past few days."

"Repairs?"

"Repairs? Ha! I wish they were. Oh, much more distressing than that," he said half to himself as he left.

There was nothing Blanch could do. She went back to typing from the document, which was as thick as when she had started. And still as pointless. Was she being criminal doing this, participating in a fraud? She hadn't thought of that before. And yet, what harm could it be, to anyone? Or, for that matter, what help? He wanted the manuscript done.

What was most curious about it was the ink. It was not fresh as it should have been. Unless he was using a bottle of old ink, if that was possible. Perhaps it was the oldness of the paper that was affecting the ink. But they seemed to have aged together.

Paxton stood at the door. Blanch sat beside a tiny elegant circular table with a mosaic top, on a swollen, tiny, horsehair-upholstered chair.

They looked at each other, Blanch realizing that whoever she was, she was looking as hard at Paxton as he at her. And then she realized this indignity and arose gasping from the wicker table at which she sat.

There was no Paxton, only an empty doorway in this stripped house that she had seen for almost no time at all, and then only as an infant, and she—it—that sat at the wicker table, now stood beside it. And a flood of poignant sorrow filled her as she realized that she was Aaron, a much younger Aaron, staring at the doorway, so empty, through which Benjamin, his son, would never return. And yet in Aaron's existence, weird and temporary though it was, in the poignant joy in being, even if only to stare and suffer, in Blanch's knowing that the Aaron she was, was dead, she found herself weeping thick tears. She thought that she had felt nothing at the death of Aaron, but now she did, sobbing profoundly.

It was later in the afternoon, she could see by her watch. She went to tidy up in the washroom under the stairs. The bottles were gone.

She stepped into the hall. In a way, perhaps it was she who should be paying Mr. Mallkin, she decided.

For what?

At home, she ate a light lunch. She suddenly felt warm, suddenly felt closer to Aaron than she ever recalled having felt, as though his presence were still in the house. Warmer than she had anticipated. She went upstairs to change her sweater. On a whim she opened the bottom drawer of her bureau, was filled with a fury she never knew she could attain. The black star was gone.

She rushed downstairs, clinging to the banister, yet knowing that it was not she who was furious, who was rushing. Was it Miss Locke? Or had that Blanch, for that was her mother's name too, already married Benjamin?

Edna, tranquil, reserved, stood at the living room window with her bird book and binoculars.

"That woman," Blanch said.

Edna turned.

"That woman. We never finished that."

Edna waited.

"You were thrown down by a woman."

"She was out the door before I could look at her," Edna assured her.

"Well?"

"What do you mean?"

"The black star is gone."

"A pity," said Edna, with a touch of the sardonic. She always held material wealth in contempt.

"I'm not so sure," Blanch said. "But I just don't like people running in."

Edna sighed. "We must take to locking the door."

"Yes," said Blanch inanely.

So things were still happening here too.

And her being Aaron, earlier. Her incarnations were becoming heterosexual!

WHEN MILAN called that night they went for a walk, gravitated toward the big house, where they strolled the great driveway.

In a way it was becoming her house, Blanch mused, or had never stopped being it. It and all its new-old people. New for her, that is. She tried to sort them out, lazily, vaguely, as she sometimes tried to before falling asleep. Paxton always seemed to come first. And of course there was her mother, Blanch Locke, her maiden name, her mother whom she saw as a young woman, who only had been a young woman, whom Blanch Stowe seemed to confuse with what must have been Blanch Inscho (Blanch Locke's grandmother and Blanch Stowe's great-grandmother). Such a mishmash of cloches and flapper dresses with the dress of the 1870s and 1880s and then 1930s and 1940s. And then there was another point of confusion. The little girl who'd been disturbed by Paxton may have been, if related, Blanch Stowe's great-grandmother, and her great-great-grandmother was Mrs. Pierson, who could have been the one who hired young Paxton. But then, Blanch Locke's mother's maiden name was Blanch Inscho, as was her mother's married name— Such confusion, with all the women named Blanch.

And then that awful thing that had happened on the beach. Not to mention the slashing of the colt. If they had happened. If there was any real indication that anything had happened. And if there was anything to superstition, could the recent burning of crosses on the sand have started things? That must have occurred before the big house was built—The Great House, as one of the Blanches called it.

She must find out when the house was built.

There seemed to be overlapping groups or pairs. Her mother and her grandmother. Her grandmother and her great-grandmother. Or great-great— Her head was swimming. Perhaps she was avoiding things again, just didn't want to think any more about it.

And all the time Blanch and Milan had been quiet, and then talking, and Blanch suddenly realized that she didn't know what she might have been saying, except that they were talking about the house and its visitants.

"I've kept something back," Blanch said. She didn't look at Milan. She told him of the mysterious woman who had thrown Edna to the floor, and of the star.

Milan stopped, furious, caught her by her arm and faced her.

"This is what's so terrible," he said.

"What?"

"What—physical force—was in the house besides you?"

Blanch yanked her arm free.

"I couldn't have!" she insisted.

"I didn't say that," he said, with agony in his voice.

"I've thought of that," she confessed. But had she really? Had she tried to face anything out? "And if it had been, I would still maintain that it wasn't me."

He chuckled despondently, a bit hysterically.

"I don't know what to make of it," he said. "I don't know if this is connected or what. But in case you don't know it, you've been staying at my place lately."

Blanch was wide-eyed.

"No. It's not that wild yet," he laughed. "But after you leave—I've never been able to paint as much or so easily before. But someone seems to be with me, watching. You haven't left a spy or chaperone, have you?"

"Milan!"

"I guess all this is just stimulating me. But I'm telling you, it feels as though someone's there."

They were approaching the highway by the south exit of the great semicircular driveway. Headlights floated slowly, turned in, the car stopped beside them. It was an old noisy compact. The driver was Mr. Mallkin.

"I'm so glad," he said intensely, "that you are using my driveway. Grounds, beach—all. They're open to you. It's nice seeing people," he added desperately.

Milan thanked him.

"Oh you mustn't. You don't know the comfort." He chatted on.

Nothing really was said. Several times Blanch, who wanted to leave, could feel that Milan did too. But Mr. Mallkin talked on desperately. Profoundly selfless, dull talk. Mad talk, so pitifully pointless.

But things became clear, when he whispered, "There's someone in the house."

"Now?" said Milan.

"At night." A long pause. "In the daytime too."

"A big house has sounds," Milan said.

"That, you may well say again," said Mr. Mallkin. "I don't know why I'm telling you my troubles."

It was surprising how much you could see of Mallkin by the light of the dashboard.

"Was anything stolen?"

"No No." Mallkin giggled a moment. "Perhaps it's a poltergeist. There are such things, aren't there?"

Blanch and Milan said nothing.

"You must come for tea, the two of you. Or for a glass of wine. In the evening. We must make a real party of it sometime. Meanwhile—"

"Do you want me to look in now?"

There was a long silence; almost weeping, Mr. Mallkin said, "Would you, dear boy?"

He was obviously terrified.

They waited while Mr. Mallkin put his car away in the extreme south outbuilding, closest to the road though still some distance from it, shut the garage door, meticulous he was indeed, then the three went to the big house.

Pale in the darkness it almost glowed, only its windows black slots.

Mr. Mallkin let them in with his key.

Blanch started for the light switch.

"No," Mr. Mallkin whispered, "please."

They stood in the hall listening, their eyes growing accustomed to what visibility there was. But for obvious creaking of an empty building there was no unusual sound.

"Come with me, softly," Mr. Mallkin said.

He had removed his shoes. Except for his dark bulk there was hardly any sound. They followed him on tiptoes up the steps, both Milan and Blanch walking lightly in sneakers. They could hardly see in the dark hall.

"Follow me!"

On tiptoe, with great speed he led them. It was an odd sight, his great bulk bobbing ahead. He paused, motioned them to follow him into a room.

A pale light came in from the window. This was the bedroom Blanch had "seen," with Mr. Mallkin and the two other men.

"There," he said, pointing at an ungainly table with slanting legs sloping out toward the floor, and a flat shelf just above the floor.

"See," said Mr. Mallkin, "those papers. They've been moved again, the lot of them. The wind couldn't have done that, they've been moved as one mass. I deliberately put them in that corner. And now they're at the other end. I am not in error, my memory is like a trap. Now who would do such a silly thing?"

He was whispering all the time as though darkness and whispering made the trio invisible.

"Let's just wait," he said. "We'll wait."

He sat in his overstuffed chair. Blanch started for the straight chair, which stood next to the door. Milan leaned against a wall.

Her black silk gown rustling about her ankles, Blanch with careful orderly short steps floated more than walked into the hall.

"Blanch!" Milan said.

There was the heavy odor of the potted hibiscus in the long hall. She came softly down the thickly carpeted stairs. It was better dark. There was comfort in darkness. And a propriety in a house where nothing would ever by chance be placed amiss; impede her walking. She went on through the great dining room, on to the conservatory. There the richness of the flowers filled her lungs like a healthy drug, a health-giving drug, a sensuous drug. People said that such effluvia could kill. But this was nonsense. No, it wasn't nonsense. But it would not kill the ruler of this domain. She went to the table, without looking, took the great medallion in her hand. And then the building moved. Not she. The rooms, halls. Up. Up. On to and through the grand second floor. On to the narrow staircase to the servants' attic. Because the staircase was at the north end, she traversed the length of the passage to the south end, stepped into a room, its window little more than a skylight.

Even as the figure on the bed sat up she raised the medallion, holding it flat in her hand, smashed down, smashed down, smashed down.

Consternation!

The staff!

She bolted the length of the hall, took the narrow staircase in great leaps. Absurd what little women can do, when one can run and plunge in these broad skirts. He bounded down the main staircase, writhed, pulled, swayed, almost danced, danced in the great hall, danced from supper to breakfast. That would fix the scoundrel. Threaten his power, would he? Oh! those dances.

Slumped, looked up.

Light flicked on, yellow light.

Her head swam for a moment, she felt limp, she was looking into the eyes of Milan, who held her by the wrists.

Her left hand hurt, it was still clutching the medallion. She turned it, saw blood and hair, gasped and choked, dropped it, even as she saw that it was clean, there was no hair and blood.

Mallkin had put the lights on. He was puffing, his grey face oily looking and wet with sweat.

Milan looked stern and gloomy. Gently he lowered her hands. She slumped toward him, walked weakly to the staircase and sat down on the steps.

"What skeleton did I uncover now?" she said.

"You're the only one who saw it all," said Milan.

"Not all. I remember leaving the room with the table—"

"Yes. You went like lightning. What a walk! As

though you were four feet taller."

"Hm!"

"Practically ran, ran down the stairs into the typing room, came tearing back. You didn't see either of us."

"Dear, dear, we had a fine time following you to the attic."

"It needn't have really occurred," Blanch said wanly.

"I should hope not. But it could maybe symbolize things. Who were you?"

"That was really strange," said Blanch, glanced wonderingly at Mallkin. "Oh well." He must have had an idea of how things were going by now. "I was wearing this long full dress, the one I think I saw at the pony's."

"The woman?" Milan said.

"Now I'm not sure.

"Remember how strong I said the person was —who was kneeling on the pony's shoulder? I felt, after the staff restrained me, or whatever it was—" She looked questioningly at Milan and Mallkin, both of whom shifted embarrassedly. "I felt that I was a male. Yet I had on this—" She looked down. "*A* dress. That's all."

"That's all!" Mallkin's eyes danced. He was thrilled no end. What excitement for a lonely bachelor. He also looked frightened. "This is remarkable. Has this been going on for some time?"

Blanch shrugged. "Yes. But I don't think involving you. I mean *in* here, but not *of* here. Oh, I don't know how to put it. For instance, have the papers been moved when I've been in the house?"

This was crucial, Blanch felt.

Mallkin thought hard, "No. As a matter of fact, no. Those things happen at night."

"Then that lets me out—I hope."

"But how thrilling! Psychic. I never dared dream something like this might occur here." His excitement waned, his face seemed to turn greyer. "But now that I'm confronted with it," he continued, "I must confess that I am a coward—"

"To live in such a big house alone?!" Blanch countered.

"No, I'm a coward. I'm frightened silly. I'm stubborn, mind you, but frightened. And now, where does this leave me? I mean, this has been an immense adventure. Yet actually," he argued with himself, apparently he'd been worrying about this for some time, "the moving of the papers on my table, let us say. It's bothersome but doesn't really seem serious. I mean," he said, with a nervous laugh, "how awful is the mere moving of some papers? Silly. One would like to know what forces there are. But I am distressed. I don't think I'm going to sleep here tonight."

"I don't blame you," said Milan.

"I'm going right into Boston and stay with friends. But only for a bit, mind you. I suppose the whole thing was rather like Don Quixote," he gloomed, "my taking this huge house. But things like this are only—" he looked appealingly at the two—"passing," the last more of a question than a statement. And then, worriedly, to Blanch, "I hope this won't deter you from continuing your typing here?"

Blanch aimed a squelching look at Milan, said, "No. Things have been pretty fine in the day-time."

Mallkin was quick to catch the qualification, or seemed to catch it, but let it pass.

He said, "There is something you could do for me, Miss Stowe."

She waited.

"I don't like to seem the prying sort. But," here he looked painfully eager and pleading, as well he might, "could you—would you be so kind—as to draw up a sort of chart of what you know that might contribute to these disturbances? Or at least, whatever view you've had of it? I'd be tre-mendously obliged to you."

Blanch nodded. "I'll make up a chart for you."

"You're so kind. And now let me drive you home."

"No thanks. The walk will do us good," Milan said.

"But I have to get the car anyway."

"No, we'll walk. Thanks awfully."

"All right—if I can't prevail on you? And let me thank you very much, Mr—?"

"Hoxha."

"Mr. Hoxha. I hope you find some interest in this."

"I do," Milan said.

He suddenly seemed much happier about the whole thing.

But not so once they got out onto the darkened driveway.

Soon they saw the lights of Mallkin's compact traveling south.

"This step has not been a good one," Milan said.

"You mean Mallkin getting in on it?"

"No. I think that's to the good. He's got a stake in this now. But do you realize that you *acted* today? It wasn't that you were actually attacking someone. But. . . ."

Blanch said, "I don't know. Maybe I ought to— I almost feel as though I should get myself committed or something. It's scary."

"I wonder if amateurs should work at this sort of thing."

"Are there professionals?" Blanch asked.

"You've got a point there," Milan agreed.

"Would you think I'm crazy to suggest this? I've got the key. Let's go back in."

She couldn't see Milan's expression in the dark.

"Okay," he said quietly.

Unconsciously they walked very softly.

As soon as they entered, they could hear it.

A pounding from above. Quietly and quickly, Milan leading, they hurried up the stairs. Up the servants' attic staircase. It was coming from the very room they had been in' earlier. It still was pounding, with a sighing, if that may be said, of metal springs, metal bedframe, a dull pounding. It didn't stop.

Blanch on his heels, Milan entered the room.

The pounding continued. It didn't get louder, but it's not stopping made it sound louder, agonizing to their nerves, this pounding that would not stop. There was laughter on the floor below, nervous, tinny laughter, which stopped the pounding, or the pounding had stopped just before it, then the scuttering of footsteps.

Milan leaned weakly against the wall. There was light flooding in from the Bay now, pale light into this room bare of all furniture. Blanch was in a cold sweat.

Reluctantly the two went down into the great hall. Their eyes had become adjusted to the interior darkness.

Both sat at the foot of the steps, next to each other.

Milan for the first time put his arm around Blanch's shoulders, a protective arm.

"Wow!" he said.

"What a house of horrors," said Blanch. "I guess when you think of it, there has been quite a crowd living in a mansion for over a hundred years. Not only guests and servants. I read somewhere that when a school girl, say the daughters of the owners of a place like this, invited a school chum to stay with her, it would involve a little army. There'd be the girlfriend, her parents, and then the father's valet and the mother's maid. So I mean mathematically, that's spreading it."

"That's spreading it," Milan agreed dourly.

Blanch sighed.

The light seemed to have gotten brighter on this darker side of the house. It was strangely exciting, as though they were seeing the world through the eyes of a color-blind animal, everything grey and flat.

"This has really been a great experiment," she said cynically. "Tonight we came to clarify things and all we did was continue what I had started. All sorts of questions are bothering me. What would have happened if we hadn't gone upstairs? Were the sounds due to happen? Was I the cause of them? The medium?"

"I think the sounds were due," Milan said. "That's what Mallkin was complaining about. Things are happening in this house."

"But did I start them?"

"I don't think so. No, really. If this house were built today, say finished last summer, with only one person staying here at night— I mean, I've worked at night in laboratories and studios, in colleges. The bigger the building the worse it is. I mean the crazy noises—I don't know."

"I'm scared," said Blanch.

Milan held her tighter.

"When you went to New York, you say you couldn't get away from it."

"No. No. It was with me in New York. And then after I left—that awful slashing incident."

"I was going to say 'coincidence' again. But this whole thing has become eerie."

"Oh Milan, I'm so sorry I involved you in all this!"

"I was involved the day I was born," Milan said. "We're both way into this."

"I feel so stupid about not knowing whom to

see. What do we do? Run to a psychiatrist and say, 'Ghosts are parading around the house and won't you come and spend a month with us?' Have you any idea what they cost?"

"I know."

"And there's nothing we can call the police in for. Oh, Milan," Blanch said, almost sobbing, "is this ever going to stop?"

Milan was too gloomy and honest to reply.

Light feet tripped down the stairs. Both jumped. Both laughed at the squeak that went with the terrified mouse. Or rat. Or who knows what? As the little thing sort of whistled in its course along the walls, and disappeared.

"Well, at least that's one thing I'm not afraid of," Blanch said.

THE NEXT morning, after Blanch had let herself into the big house, she suddenly realized that she was indeed alone in it and, strangely enough, that she had never feared being alone in it. Her bad scares had occurred when others were about. And despite an attempt to activate her imagination, she felt that she couldn't fear it now, or stubbornly wouldn't, and she wondered if it weren't fact that her people had owned this place at one time that made her so self-assured.

And what a challenge, she felt all businesslike. She would make a résumé for Mr. Mallkin. As a matter of fact, it was high time she did it for herself, instead of sloppily mooning about these things. But of course it would be on his time, let him pay for it. She wondered what clutching merchant she must have descended from, but didn't let the thought distress her.

Well, here goes.

She wished that she were an artist and could paint the people she recalled.

She decided that she would work backwards in time.

Her hands poised at the type keys, she suddenly realized that she would have to get dates and things. It was silly to start with nothing.

She literally ran to the front door, on the way she wondered if she had shut the conservatory door or not.

The refectory door?

She had shut—for that matter, under the new policy had locked—the outer door. It was open now.

Oh God!

"Mr. Mallkin!" she called upstairs. "Mr. Mallkin!"

There was no answer.

Angrily she slammed the door shut. She hurried along the driveway, saw that all the doors on the outbuildings were open.

No, no, she could not be sure of that. She wasn't rationalizing to herself, she had had this difficulty before.

She rushed home, knocked on Edna's door. She entered, sat on Edna's bed.

"I need some dates and things."

Edna put aside the book she had been reading, waited.

"Just these dates. I was born in 1946. Mother died in 1947. When was she born?"

"In 1926."

"My father—when was he born?"

"Benjamin was born in 1921."

"Now. Do you know when Grandma Locke was born?"

"She was born in 1900."

"And when did she die?"

"She died in 1945."

"She was really young then, wasn't she?"

"Yes."

Edna certainly wasn't one to go overboard speaking.

"What did she die of?"

"She drowned."

"Where?"

"I believe it was near Newport."

"Oh. And Mr. Locke. My grandfather."

"He died within a year." Edna could not escape Blanch's questioning look, added, "In a boating accident."

Blanch thrilled. "Drowned too?"

"I don't know."

"Where?" Blanch asked.

"They had given up the house. But it was right off here."

"Oh. That takes care of the Lockes. And before that—the Inschos."

"Blanch Inscho, your great-grandmother—"

"Now this is still on mummy's side."

"Yes. Blanch Inscho was born in 1870. That is, that was her wedded name. She married Ian Inscho."

"Was she an only child?"

"Even as your mother and grandmother." Suddenly, although Edna's face didn't freeze or harden, Blanch could see that set look of inexorable integrity settle on her grandmother's features. "There was reference to possibly another child," Edna said very slowly, as if struggling to recall.

"And Blanch Inscho would be the daughter of—?"

"Your great-great—yes, your great-great-grandmother who was a Pierson."

Not smiling, but with a voice a little less rigid than it had been, Edna said, "When I was a girl, Mrs. Pierson was in her sixties, and she lived well into her seventies."

"What was she like?"

"It's hard to say. I don't think I saw her more than half a dozen times, and then not closely. At church and hospital bazaars and functions of that sort. She was, I believe, one of the strongest women I have ever seen. It was more than appearance. I remember at one bazaar—it was just for a moment—her helping carry a platform. There were sturdy young men struggling at one end and she, unruffled, at the other. We were all surprised."

"It doesn't seem to have gone into the blood, does it?" Blanch said ruefully.

"As a matter of fact, no," said Edna. "She

seemed to be more like some of her servants than her own family. Mr. Pierson, like Mr. Inscho, and Mr. Locke, were all in business in Boston, I think in stocks and shares. They were almost like guests in the house. One never heard about them. But I can't say, I had no access to them."

Edna stopped speaking and waited, seemed to know what she was waiting for.

Blanch said, "Benjamin?"

"Aaron was the son of Myra Stowe."

Blanch started. What an odd answer!

"But Myra—"

"No. That was Myra's maiden name. The family goes by—the family such as it is—goes by Myra's name."

"And his father?"

"Aaron and his mother were abandoned, probably before he was born."

"By whom?"

"I do not know. His birth record describes him as the son of Aaron Stowe, with his mother's maiden name Myra Stowe."

"Well, they could be cousins."

"I asked Aaron about it and he said no, there had been another name. In her later years Mrs. Stowe destroyed her marriage license and since we don't know where they were married, this is all we know."

"And you?"

"I am descended from as thin a line as everyone else we have been speaking about. From an Ulster Quaker, a tailor, who settled in Pennsylvania with William Penn, and his succession of Quaker artisans."

They sat in silence for some time. This was as much as Blanch had ever heard from Edna. And despite what Edna had said, at no time did Blanch feel that she was opening up any wells of reminescence.

At last Blanch said to Edna, "I suppose you're wondering why I'm asking you all these questions now."

But Edna wasn't. "Such curiosity is not unusual. Especially after a death."

A long silence followed.

"I think," Blanch finally said, terribly nervous and embarrassed and somewhat ashamed, "I've been seeing some of these people." She was going to say "in my mind's eye," but that would be a lie, directly or by implication.

For once Blanch witnessed Edna doing a consciously cruel thing.

Edna said, "I have no truck with such concepts." It was cruel because there was almost a smile on her firm old lips. Faith can have its arrogance too.

Must be her sin for the decade, Blanch decided.

Edna picked up her book and waited, a pointed hint for Blanch to leave.

Blanch left.

THE NEXT WAS a murky morning. The strange
"stilt" walk had returned. She glanced back—to
find the door she could have sworn she had shut,
wide open. She recalled Edna saying she must
lock the door now and started back, but felt too
weak to climb the steps. Angrily she turned and
stubbornly went on to the big house, down the
foggy road.

It was as if smog had mysteriously descended
on the Cape within the greyness, with nimbuses
about the trees that didn't make the light lighter, but the trees dirtier looking.

She felt old, stiff-legged, bitter. She tortured
herself, as much as she could think in this grey
dullness that seemed to have entered her brain,
with the knowledge or feeling that this was a
downgrade, that there was no stopping her de-
scent to greater dullness, darkness, vague bitter-
ness, that there was no stopping her going to do
what she was going to do, whatever that was and
however unwilling she was to do it. Then, near
where the lane intersected with the narrow highway, she saw a tall figure waiting. It might have
been a caped figure, it might have been—that
awful person, always waiting for her.

It seemed to be waiting for all the Blanches. All
the Blanches—

Mrs. Pierson—no one had said she was a
Blanch.

Waiting for all the Blanches.

She found herself meekly continuing as though had she known this would be her death she would have had to continue up this lane, this road. It was hardly a relief to see, there had been no transition from Paxton to Milan, Milan standing there, what she had thought a cape was Milan's rain slicker thrown over his shoulders.

She continued on. Milan did not gesture to her. And yet it was almost assault, the way he stood his ground, with no play, no friendliness, no recognition. And Blanch—who felt as grey as her stilt walk, the walk of an old woman, rheumatic or arthritic—approaching, felt no love, no hope, in Milan; in her mental blankness had no recollection of their eager curiosity of the day before. She tried, barely tried, or almost tried to hark back to the thrills and laughter they had had together. But what little appeared, of place or action, not emotion, was as grey now and flat as the refectory, the empty hall, her empty life.

He did not come to meet her.

At last she stood before him, her chin angled up toward his face.

Milan seemed to be struggling to say something very serious, very unpleasant to her.

Finally he did speak, said, "Blanch, you've got to stop going—you've got to not go—today or ever."

And yet, whatever success he intended to have, if any, she could not escape seeing that he was losing as he was speaking to her.

She said nothing.

"Good God, Blanch!" he said. "You don't want to solve anything. You keep dragging yourself back to some sacrificial altar. What do you expect to find after all the months you've been looking? What you find will be either another period of time, where you'll lose what we live in now—or you'll walk into something that's been waiting to get at you. Blanch, please—you're not listening to me."

She stood silent, looking up at him.

"Well, defend yourself. Tell me that I'm a fool."

The saving looseness began to embrace her knees.

This had been a bad period. She walked to the side of the road, leaned against a tree. Suddenly she burst into tears, silly hysterical tears. She was terribly embarrassed by the childishness of her tears, and was especially dismayed because she knew that Milan was taking it as a reproach.

"Oh I'm a nut!" he said, "but Blanch, can't you understand how committed I am? I mean, to you. Damn, I'm not too flush. But we'll go away together, we'll sweat it out. We'll work it out somehow."

Blanch found herself blessedly relieved, her face moist, her lips salty, but fresh, against the thing that made her a stilt-walker a moment before.

"I mean—we'll get married," he said, unwittingly making it sound like an unpleasant necessity, an afterthought.

What a proposal!

With glistening, wet eyes, "Milan," she said, "I'm not that snotty. But if I'm—" she dared, "if I'm to be anything to you, I'm not coming to you damaged."

Milan seemed almost weeping. Yes, there were tears in his eyes.

"What kind of talk is this? We've got nothing to—"

Suddenly in all her love, Blanch felt an alien but identifiable hardness in her, that of Edna, as she said, "I'm not going to romanticize this. Either I'm fighting myself or something other than myself. But I am not myself, I'm not totally myself until these things get settled once and for all."

"But it's been dragging on."

"That's it. It's been as though I've been walking under water, isn't it? I think I've felt that way all my life."

Water. Sudden images. Her mother, her father. The Lockes, separately. They whipped past her mind. One must have attachments to move in definite directions. Blanch realized now that she never had an attachment—until Milan.

She looked assessingly at him, but gently. She could have said, she heard herself saying, *'You know, I've been wrong from the start. I've never had attachments.'* But she had become so adept at moving swiftly in time that she stood outside herself at this moment, outside of the statement, in fact it had not been made and she was going to stop it before it could be made, because that would have appealed to his kindness.

He handed her a crumpled wad of Kleenex—
an appurtenance no painter in acryllic is without
today.

She dried her nose, eyes, with her back to him,
then turned to him. "Thanks for blocking me this
morning, for awhile. What made you come out?"

"Ever since that typing thing, I don't know—I
don't know if I can live in that place any more.
It's just the darndest hanging doom. I'm not jok-
ing. And I'm not psychic. But I never ran into
anything like this. There's been the strangest atmosphere in the cottage. And damn it, I think
I'm beginning to hear things. Something is really
cooking."

Blanch said, "We've been at this all so long.
Milan, look, it seems to be reaching some sort of a
climax. Why don't we face it out? Why don't we
hit it today? Let's hope it's not that tough. Maybe
we'll get an answer. And maybe we'll get—"
Blanch shrugged. "Could anything be worse, in a
way, than this crazy tormenting and torturing
that's been going on?"

"Your walk as you were coming toward me—"

"That's right. Maybe it's me, maybe it's the
house. It's time we settled that, isn't it?"

"But—"

"Please. Come on the job with me. I'll tell you
what. You go behind the outbuildings, I'll go up
the drive. As soon as I get in, I'll open a north
window in the conservatory. Spy on me, hide
from me, whatever you want."

Milan seemed to hesitate.

This was asking so much of him. She looked at him pleadingly, knowing that he would be absolutely right in turning that down—in turning her down.

He was quick, caught the look. "I'm not thinking of me. I just don't want anything to happen to you."

He reached his hand out, even as she did hers. They clasped hands tightly.

A smile, a hesitant smile sneaked to his lips.

"I never did avoid a fight," he said, with comic ruefulness.

It was wonderful walking with him again, only he seemed to be marching more than walking. With all his friendliness, he seemed terribly angry and determined. Blanch felt how awful she'd feel if she were someone Milan was at war with. And wondered with a shiver if a solution of some of the terrible things that seemed to be hinted at might not send him against her.

"You're a stubborn cookie," he said fondly.

As they approached the big house, Blanch said, "I'm just in a rut. I think I've always been in ruts."

"Well, as soon as I can, I'm going to get you out of them."

"For new ruts?" She wondered if she were kidding.

"Shut up," he said, hurt.

He remained on the highway as she started into the drive. She turned, looked at him questioningly.

"Don't worry," he said softly, "just keep going."

She smiled, shrugged, went on to the building.

He was probably running along the outside of the wall, she suspected.

Almost immediately the cold seized her joints and bones. She was furious with herself, with nature seeming to collaborate with the morbid by supplying this foul weather, dirty air and low sky. This was really the "pathetic fallacy": "the weeping willow," "the angry sea," she ruminated half jokingly, as she put her hand on the great bronze doorknob. It felt clammy and strangely soft, almost like flesh. She shuddered, pushed the door open, stepped in.

The house was silent, the light dirty, dirtier than it should have been with as much light as there was outside.

At least she was walking all right. "There is no such thing as *minor* surgery," she remembered the statement. Well, she had had surgery. And that actress who had gotten over so much worse. She shut the door softly, almost sprang out of her shoes at its slam.

Totally unnerved, shivering, she started to the refectory. She was furious that she was wearing loafers with leather heels and soles, the terrible clacking in the empty house making the silence more silent, ominous. Of all the fool things to have worn. She clacked—oh if she could only stop clack clack clacking—through the refectory into the conservatory.

It was almost as though clouds of darkness hung over the long, laden tables, over the typing stand.

She would open the window for Milan, the one behind her typing chair. Then he could come at any time, witness anything, climb in if he wished.

She found herself in the typing chair, switching on the typing lamp. What a small weak nimbus of light for her type copy. Was the electric power weak? How darker the darkness around it. Had she opened the window?

Three quick clacks of her footsteps in the refectory. They couldn't be, she was sitting where she was. Silence. Had the footsteps occurred?

She began typing. She must have opened the window, to feel a presence, his presence of course, behind her.

> horse-power, multiply the figures in the table by two. For any other loss of pressure, multiply by the square root of the given loss. For any other length of pipe, *divide 240 by the given length expressed in diameters, and multiply the figures in the table by the square root of this quotient,* which will give the flow for one lb. loss of pressure. Conversely, dividing

It was a comfort, with the new under-butler, a great comfort. She found that she didn't have to resist, that she had always been resisting, even in her immolations in time. But now there was compliance. He would do the worrying. Indeed, he would protect her. With his long face and handsome auburn hair and distinguished bearing. She of the prune-colored sateen frock, button shoes, the tightness of the sash about her hourglass waist. With him there was security. Less than fear itself, and not a mere absence of fear. He would fend for her. Though she would taunt him too as, no one looking, she skipped up the steps of the great staircase.

And even as she gamboled up, there were moments of—not the awareness of danger—but the awareness of the fact that there would have been danger were he not following her closely, she not seeing, he not to be seen. She did not turn.

On the first landing she saw the massive pear-shaped back view of Mr. Mallkin walking toward the south window, and she looked close, or rather looked harder. Mallkin continued, lumbering toward the end of the hall, seemingly unaware of anyone observing him. And the girl observing him, the girl following him, was not Blanch, but an ancient Blanch with a trim yet sturdy, hard figure. If she was a Blanch. Or perhaps Mrs. Pierson?

She heard herself, whoever she was, sigh despairingly, and then that wild gaiety seemed to return, and the Blanch in the prune-colored frock was running up the stairs *to* him, while today's Blanch wondered how he could be both before and behind her.

Because of the bleakness of the sparsely furnished servants' rooms, the doors open by order as in a prison or barracks, with almost no personal possessions on the bureaus, each cot prim and pale; the windows with the thinnest white curtains—the one door shut was all the more significant.

As Blanch of today she walked. As the woman or girl in the prune-colored dress she bounded, frolicked; simultaneously there was a drag of caution and unwillingness, and the speedy, gay flight. As she approached, she felt that she had reached the solution of so much, an open door that was truly open, that would reveal all that she had known. As she moved toward his room, which was on the east side of the house, with some hunger, the desire for some meeting, she suddenly cannily paused. The light naturally was strongest, at this hour, from the east, entering the bright bare room that she had not reached, making a shadow of the figure standing just inside the doorway.

The girl in the prune dress ran to it. Blanch of today not quite conscious, not quite reasoning, but Blanch retaining some of her personality, braked strongly, resisting, slowing but not stopping the progress toward the door. A feeling of danger, possibly emotional, or even worse—moral, helped her to struggle backwards, as though fighting cords that were drawn about her shoulders and pulled her toward the shadow of the figure that threw its silhouette across the floor. It was almost beyond her fighting, and yet she would not surrender. Prune-colored forward, Blanch back. Suddenly with all her force she screamed long and loud. Whether it were a sound or a silent agony, almost at once the shadow burst from the room as she spun for flight, and behind her, he whom she had thought was security, was Paxton. She screamed running at this new figure, fighting, insanely terrified at the awareness that this was Paxton, Paxton too, as she beat with clenched fists against the stiff cloth, the hard chest. There was a roar, a wind-like rush, at the movement of a body behind her, the shadow from the room. Even as Paxton attacked, his face twisted with fury, his giant backhand flying toward her and smacking her violently across the cheek and bridge of the nose, she screamed, she struggled, she ducked, broke under his left armpit, rushed to the stairs screaming and weeping, scrambled down sobbing, flying from step to step, clutching at the banister, rushing to the bottom, absolutely winded and shattered, and disbelieving too, although this had been much too tangible. She nodded weakly, sobbing for breath, against the great door.

She threw the door open, staggered out, aimlessly wandered north on the path beside the windows, felt suddenly impelled to turn.

Milan. He was in—

She gasped low.

Milan lay sprawled before the north window. Silent, inert, his face buried in the grass.

He had never even entered. Blanch's own

world reeled. She felt a terrible sense of loss. Hopelessly she lurched to the form before her, too saddened to even whimper as she tugged at his shoulders. But even as she felt their reassuring heat and strength he shook his head, sighed as he sat up, his back against the building.

"Milan! Milan!"

"Ooh my head!"

"You—"

Blanch arose, and another Blanch turned and screamed, one long agonized gut wail.

Who had been in the conservatory behind her? followed her up the stairs? And all too tangible.

But there had been no scream. She had committed herself too much, had too much pride, perhaps duplicity.

Milan arose, sort of climbing up the wall with his back against it, propelled by the palms of his hands, shook his head again ruefully, took a few steps.

"People," she said.

"What do you mean?"

"Oh, this is real," she said, "this is real," and found herself terribly angry.

Her fists clenched. She wanted to run back in. He caught her wrist.

"Wait a minute," he said.

"Don't you want to get them?"

"I don't know how to say it," he said. "But no —no real person hit me."

"But you were hit?"

"Yes. I was hit."

"Well somebody had to—."

"Not anybody. No."

"How can you tell?"

"I just know."

"What about my face?" she said.

He studied it. "What about it?"

"Come on! Anything about the color?"

"Either you used rouge on one side—"

"Somebody smacked me," she said.

"You can say that again." Milan smiled wryly. "I hope you got at him."

"Why do you say that?"

"I wonder if you really know yourself."

"I don't know," said Blanch. "I don't know." Then, "You never came in!"

He pointed to the window with his chin. It was closed.

"That gives it a new dimension," she said.

"What do we do now?"

Now she was unsure. She had asked for a lot and gotten a lot and she was no closer. But this was a totally new frame of action.

"You're going back to typing," said Milan, matter-of-factly. The caveman had committed himself, to hunt or kill.

"Well, I don't know—with the window."

"I'm going in with you."

Silently the two returned.

Oh no! The door was shut.

"I left it open," she said querulously.

"That should be the least of your troubles," Milan said quietly.

They stepped inside. Both inadvertently looked up.

Mr. Mallkin stood on the landing with his hands on the railing, looking down.

"Anything unusual happen?" said Blanch.

"Noises?" said Mr. Mallkin.

"Yes."

"About the usual," he said quietly. "Nothing more."

She wondered what the usual was, had an idea, then said, "Mr. Hoxha is going to be with me in the conservatory."

"Feel free to come, go, stay," Mr. Mallkin said petulantly. He seemed tired, defeated. He turned. "Well," he said, "I must be . . ." Nothing more. He walked off.

There was a flutter as of feet, just as they stepped into the refectory.

"What's that?" Milan said.

"Par," Blanch replied cynically.

It had gotten still darker. It hardly could be called day.

"How's your head?" Blanch said.

"Never been KO'd before. Surprisingly not bad. Guess it's my ego more than anything else. That was really—I don't know. You'd better type," he said.

Blanch sat at the typewriter. But didn't type.

Milan leaned against the wall, slid down to the floor, sat with his back to the wall, his knees almost to his chin.

"What happened?" Milan asked.

Blanch told. Briefly, accurately, not a word or recollection wasted.

"In a way, things are kind of shaping up," he

said. "At least the picture seems to be filling out."

". . . So I ran up to meet him. But I suppose I also thought he was behind me. It was crazy. And then it was Paxton I met, yet Paxton was behind me too—Paxtons all around."

"This other butler. You thought he was sort of me?"

"Yes."

A hideous thought, that beating—if it had occurred. Paxton attacking his competitor? Or she —*a* Blanch, that is—attacking Paxton? Or someone she thought was Paxton. But hadn't it been a strong man who had wielded the medallion? Someone disguised as a—she couldn't remember. Her brain seemed all crawly. Or rather foggy, with swatches of cloud and mist that she suspected she didn't want drawn aside.

"My God!" Milan roared, "then who was in the room?"

She shivered. For there had also been someone other than Milan in the conservatory.

"When I'm jumping around in three generations," Blanch replied in answer to Milan's question about the attic room, "I don't see why there have to be any relationships between who was behind me and who was before me. It could be the same person."

"You mean the man in the room upstairs really was Paxton?"

"Why couldn't there be two or three Paxtons?" Blanch said. "He worked in the family for two generations—three generations. And are we always the same person? From day to day, from year to year?"

Milan waited.

"When I was a little girl—or one of me!—I went to where I shouldn't have gone, the servants' quarters. He had a right to stop me. Or were there several such visits? And this last time, was it the same girl who went to the attic? Or her daughter?"

"Maybe there was something going on and maybe it was innocent," Milan suggested. "But I still don't dig this violence."

Poor Milan. He had really become part of it. First poor Edna, thrown to the floor! Then Blanch, who'd just been worked over upstairs, her cheek still hurt. And Milan, knocked unconscious. The lines of battle were drawn.

"I mean," he argued, "maybe the things that happened at times—for you, or before you, or before whatever you temporarily had become— didn't happen. There's always that possibility. You know—the hopes, the dreams, the desires of the people who lived here. Maybe they didn't occur. Maybe, without running you down, some sort of a—"

"That's interesting," Blanch assured him. "Some sort of a network of things I've never faced. The awful dreams and tendencies that are supposed to be in everybody's subconscious."

"That's right. Not only yours. That of other people."

But at least the picture was filling out—whatever it was.

Something else was filling out. In the southeast corner of the room, where there seemed to be no reason for reflection, a dirty cloud of pale light was beginning to develop and build itself, increase, with a sort of face one sees on the moon yet doesn't see, only more gaseous. Blanch, pale, had risen, was watching it. Milan rose. Did he see it too? As though somebody had stepped away, or slid from the edge of her vision, the cloud with its face began to dissolve.

Suddenly there was an ear-shattering mass of door-slamming all over the house, above, below, slamming, presumably opening, slamming, doors slamming wildly, a tattoo, a flurry, a crescendo of slams. Blanch followed Milan as he ran through the refectory, but not before she noticed the way Milan glanced at the now empty corner—he too had seen the face.

They ran into the great hall. Just as they reached it, the door-slamming ceased and a great many-throated agonized sad moan welled up through the building.

Sick with guilt for what poor Mr. Mallkin must be suffering, she ran to his door, knocked on it, knocked again. There was no answer.

She opened the door and entered. The room was as they had seen it before, but unoccupied.

Blanch walked to the window, glanced over the wide lawn and driveway. A single car was passing on the darkened highway. An ordinary, everyday thing, and yet even that seemed sinister in this madness within which Blanch and now Milan were living.

Was death indeed so evil a thing? Everything she had encountered, now she realized, had been awful, and made her think of—was it the Hopi Indians?—who wouldn't accept Christianity because they would not accept the Holy Ghost. The Indians felt that everything of the dead was evil, inimical, and they tried not to think of them, never referred to them, Blanch thought that most people were probably good and lived happy lives, or relatively good and relatively happy, and that when they died they simply ended, or rested, or were transferred elsewhere. Except for those figures who had been peopling her other life for the past weeks—they seemed held back by some monstrous evil within whose circumference she now moved.

"I still think," said Blanch, "that all we need is a breakthrough. That all we have to do is find something that's been concealed here, to stop this —this haunting, whether you believe in such things or not. I know I didn't."

With a rueful smile Milan said, "I'm not going to argue. I've developed some changed attitudes lately."

"Now what?" She was wondering if he would again deter her from danger. But he must have been won over.

"That flurry of noises was really crazy though, wasn't it?" he said.

Blanch shuddered. More of that, and she thought perhaps she would lose her mind.

"Come on," Milan said.

They left, she following him to the attic servants' quarters. All the doors were shut, with pale light from the small window at each end of the corridor.

Milan opened each of the doors. The rooms were empty, room after room. Each identical, like photo prints from one negative, yet each— The last door was thrown open.

There sat Paxton. Neatly, dryly dressed, a largely black outfit, a noble mane of white hair, a wall-eye.

Blanch felt her knees turn to water.

Milan sagged to the doorframe.

Such malevolence! Such incredible hatred. On the face of—no one. The room was empty.

Blanch turned to Milan. There was no need to ask if he had seen.

"I'll be!" Milan said. "I'll be!"

Both left the empty room, descended, left the big house.

It was still a strangely dark lowering day. Blanch looked at her watch.

"It's after one."

Milan seemed incapable of speech.

"Let's go to my place for a snack," Blanch said.

Milan looked at her in amazement. "You're fantastic!" he said.

She shrugged. What else was there to do?

The two strolled through the obscuring, electricity-charged twilight of the day.

"This is fascinating," Milan said. He seemed to have recovered. "Amazing."

Blanch said nothing.

Once inside, Blanch hurried to Edna's room, knocked on the door, was asked to come in.

She said to Edna, "Do you know anything about Paxton. He was the head butler, or butler, for years."

Edna paused for a moment, said, "No."

THEY WERE too excited to eat much. But suddenly really in unison, Blanch felt a new strength. They started back immediately after lunch.

"Whatever happened to Mallkin?" Milan asked.

"He's probably run to Boston again."

"Oh, oh," said Milan.

The day was still dark, the sort of New England darkness that makes one feel there never had been, never would be, sunlight. As they approached the house, they could not take their eyes off what Milan had noted, the front door.

"Did we leave it open?" he asked.

"That," said Blanch, "is totally immaterial." She thought of all the portal traumas that had beset her recently.

They went directly to the conservatory.

"Do you want to start right in?"

"No," Blanch said.

Milan laughed. "I don't blame you."

Again he sat on the floor. Blanch was in the chair.

"Oh yes. Today—when we ran out. Did you see that light—that sort of face—in the corner?"

Milan's jaw set. Was he avoiding her eyes?

"No," he said.

"Oh." Then, "What about in the next room?" The refectory.

"What?"

"When we went running upstairs. That sort of —blip—in the corner of the eye?"

Milan nodded.

"Let's look around," he said.

The darkness had not abated. If anything, it was thicker, despite the time of day.

Looking about the refectory, Milan said, "Have you ever seen this as a banquet hall? I mean, beside that meeting we horned in on?"

"I think as a—you know—a Blanch."

In the great hall they looked about. Nothing to see really. One immediately encompasses emptiness. Or perhaps there was something to see.

Yes. The door to the south room was shut. Milan tried it.

"That's funny," he said. It was locked.

They went outside to try to look through the window. The shades were drawn.

They returned to the house, after opening the door they thought they had left open.

"Wow!" said Milan. He didn't have to add,

"I'm getting that way too."

On the second floor they looked into the bedrooms. Merely the cots that were presumably used the night of the party.

Mr. Mallkin's door was still unlocked. Unhesitatingly Milan entered, with Blanch following.

The curtain before the clothes rack didn't conceal the several identical suits, the overcoat.

Blanch looked closely at the bed, saw none of the slashes she had seen being made in one of her "visits." She slid her hand under the worn patchwork quilt, suddenly whipped it back. There had been slashes, now repaired with wide surgical tape. Not very comfortable to lie on, she decided.

And of course had she really seen the vandalism, in a sort of *déjà vu*, with the fellow sitting on the bed?

"I can't understand it," said Milan, looking at the books in the bookcase. "I don't think he bought these books. I mean singly. They must just be bunches from the Salvation Army secondhand shops. I mean, not just one book at a time. There's no sense. It's like you see them on the store shelves, jumbled together, no selection." At the table he said, "I don't know that he reads this stuff. Look at the same goofy mixture. Look at the dust on the top books. What sort of a life can he lead here? What's he doing?"

Blanch shrugged and rolled her eyes.

Milan left the room, Blanch following him. Milan took her hand.

It was worth almost all the troubles. She

couldn't remember anyone showing such affection to her before. Not even Tod. But then, she and Milan certainly had a lot in common now.

"The smell," Blanch said.

"What?"

"From the end of the hall." The south end. "Can't you smell it? The hibiscus?"

"Maybe I can. But how could you . . . ?"

"I've seen it." Sardonically, "I think I've watered it."

Oh no! Four solid steps above. Leather heel and leather sole.

It was a very businesslike Milan who started back the whole length of the hall. The staircase to the attic was at the north end.

As they passed the balconylike section, with the great hall below, they saw that the door was open. They hurried up the attic stairs.

The silence was total. Feeling impelled, Blanch entered the center, east bedroom, went to the window, looked down at the Bay balcony. A still, silent black figure leaning with its elbow, on the rail.

"Look," Blanch whispered.

Milan did.

"Ssh," he said.

Tiptoeing both ran down, ran along the second floor corridor to the French windows leading to the Bay balcony.

It was empty.

Hallucination built for two.

"We're running around like a couple of

kooks," Milan said. "We're not getting anywhere. We're not answering anything by following every time they want us to."

He said this, as aimlessly they descended the stairs. As aimlessly, Blanch tried the door to the south room. It was unlocked.

"Can you beat that?" she said.

They entered.

It was empty but for an elaborate dusty dining table, not more than eight feet long, with several chairs about it.

Dispiritedly Milan sat down. Blanch took the chair opposite him.

"It's funny," Milan said. "Earlier, when all hell broke loose, we were fresh."

"And now," Blanch said, seeing the gist.

"Nothing, really."

"Maybe," said Blanch. "But I've felt this piling of one thing on top of another. Do you think maybe," she said, looking into Milan's eyes, "since poltergeists are supposed to come from a person who is present—"

"But," said Milan, "I don't think that works."

"With me?"

"Yes."

"Why?"

"I think Mallkin had those noises without you around."

"That's a relief. I'm going to knock off for the day."

"I don't blame you," Milan said.

Edna was leaving the kitchen, looked compassionately at Blanch as she entered.

What was there to say?

Blanch went to her room. She felt numbed with the experiences of the past few months, incapable of thinking ahead. The night was fitful.

BLANCH FOUND herself up at dawn. The sky was of a bright fair flesh tint, the sun sparkling clear, the air sweet and exhilarating. The troubled past day and night had disappeared under the bright smudge of nature's thumb. The awful noises, blows—all such madness—shrunk to nothing before the sweet realism of a Cape morning at its best.

Blanch showered cold, something not her habit, threw on a tweed skirt, sweater and jacket, went down to the kitchen, laughed as she looked out of the window, threw open the back door and ran out. Milan, who had been approaching the house, stopped and looked at her, his face as bright as the sky. Both burst into laughter.

Still laughing, Blanch said, "Gosh, I hope we don't wake up the neighborhood."

"You too," Milan said. "This is really crazy, isn't it? Wow, what weather! Shall we dump the job? Let's bomb the house."

Blanch laughed. "I'm starving and hate my cooking."

"They've opened the old diner down the road.

I think it's the only trucker's place between here and Maine."

There they had grapefruit, wheat cakes and sausages, eggs and coffee. About all they could do was laugh and smile at each other. The weather was just too right.

Then gradually their early rising, the dirty light of the diner with its mephitic atmosphere, dampened their spirits.

As they left, Blanch said, "Real schizos. Up and down, up and down."

"You mean manic-depressives."

"Whatever they are."

"You felt it too?" said Milan.

"Well, sure," said Blanch.

They were in Edna's Dart on the way back. Blanch wasn't surprised, though nothing had been said, when they drew up before the big house.

It was only 7:30. The front door was open.

"I thought he was going to lock it," Milan said.

"Yeah."

They were in a rut. They entered.

The moment they entered they could feel the emptiness. The added emptiness. The forsaken emptiness. Before, the house had been empty with a sense of waiting. Now it felt abandoned.

In the conservatory Blanch gasped. The manuscript she had been copying from, the pages she had typed out, the unfinished page, all were gone. But directly before the table, and they could smell the ashes, was a metal trash can. The ashes of the work, she was sure, were in the can.

On the table was an envelope containing Blanch's pay for the hours she had worked that week, and an added twenty-five dollars, obviously a bonus.

"Hm. Sounds terminal," Milan said.

"Severance pay."

They climbed the stairs to the second floor, entered Mallkin's room. His suits were gone, the bureau drawers open and empty. On the bed, on the tattered patchwork quilt, lay the crystal star and beside it a note in Mallkin's scrawly handwriting:

Why this?

That was all Blanch needed, another mystery. She disregarded the star and the note and automatically they left the room to climb to the attic floor.

The rooms were empty as ever. Blanch looked down to the Bay balcony.

"That's the way it's supposed to be," Milan said. It was empty.

"And that's been the exception lately," Blanch said dourly.

And then relaxed to enjoy the view. The wonderful light and air. The Bay seemed so immense, the house chastened despite its dimensions inside. Blanch knew that from the outside there would be little indeed, the house shrunk against the landscape, seascape—a pimple, a zero.

"No cross on the beach," Milan said. He turned

to Blanch and said, "I think maybe this is it."

Blanch felt relaxed, felt that she had returned to the world, somehow felt that the impositions, whatever their source, had stopped. But she did not feel relieved. There had been too many surprises.

"Well," Milan said, as they started down.

The great hall seemed to shake with a shriek, a strangled cry. Blanch shuddered, almost fainted, then felt suddenly alert, terribly alert, and with some satisfaction, for it was a real alertness, a physical, determined alertness and not a despairing reception.

"That's one place we've never been," said Milan with surprise, the two running into the kitchen.

"There must be, there's bound to be—" said Blanch. "Unless it's an airspace."

Milan opened closet door after closet door in the great kitchen. One door opened in—but was locked.

Milan squared off, raised one of his long powerful legs, with great force kicked hard beside the doorknob, limped, smiled sheepishly.

"They didn't make them the way they do in the movies," he said.

"It's the new realism. Now they kick two and three times." Blanch was speaking from the other end of the kitchen, where she removed a skeleton key from one of the closet doors.

"What a cluck!" Milan said of himself.

The bolt in the cellar door turned smoothly.

The air was surprisingly dry and odorless.

They went down the dark steps. At the foot they reached faint light, from the dirty pale overgrown windows on the Bay side.

How little they had seen of the house from the Bay side. It's always the ugly side you seem to live most with, Blanch decided.

Milan had been clouted only the day before. Now he stood with his ankles apart, his knees slightly bent, his shoulders and elbows ready.

It had impressed both simultaneously. Blanch found her hands becoming fists. Someone stood in the dark far corner of the basement.

Tight physical fear. Blanch could feel the cold on her back, on the nape of her neck, her skull crawling, as she approached with Milan.

A very dark figure, and pale face. They drew closer to it. It stood silent, immobile. It was so dark that despite the paleness of its face they had to approach further to see it, beyond caution, until they were inches from it, yet felt they might have to come even closer.

It was Paxton.

But something had changed in this iron, distant face, with the great scar on its forehead. Poor Paxton.

For this was the face, the form, of someone who had lived but now did not. A form, a face, yet no more than a tomb inscription, a name and date scrawled on a flyleaf. At most, perhaps, the still uncovered dead face, with its mortician-painted elevations and depths of dead flesh. No, not even that. A sigh that had no longer sound, an inscription that had faded to nullity. A face that had become, not ordinary, his features were too handsome, but clay.

Blanch and Milan stole a startled look at each other, then glanced back to find themselves standing absurdly close to a corner of the house's foundation, with nothing else before them.

The walleye, the white hair, the strong face. Would they see them again?

Quietly, as though at the end of a church service, they returned to the kitchen. Milan shut the basement door.

As they were leaving by the front door, something drew Blanch to the south room. She put her hand on Milan's arm. They opened the door and entered.

The blinds were still drawn. Edna sat at the table.

In the soft light she seemed younger.

"Come sit down," she said.

They sat at the table.

"After all these years," Edna said, "I discovered that I too have vanity. I held off telling you something discreditable about our family, feeling that it wouldn't matter in the long run. But last night I was drawn to your door. I stood and listened. You were so disturbed that I knew I was doing a wrong."

Was that why Blanch had arisen with such a sense of relief this morning?

"In closing the estate of your father, Aaron discovered something from which—I won't say he never recovered. But he was never the same again."

Edna, who had been holding herself tight, sat back. With a quiet, ironic smile that was unfamiliar to Blanch, she went on.

"Sigmund Freud says that although we may not inherit the morality of our fathers, we do inherit their feelings of guilt." And then, more to the point, "Aaron discovered who his father was, that the family was not Stowe, as I've already told you, but that the true name was of a butler from this house."

"Well—" Milan began to minimize.

Edna interrupted him. "It isn't a matter of our democratic leanings, Mr. Hoxha. Unfortunately it became a matter of eugenics."

Blanch suddenly understood so much, suspected that she had understood more all along than she had been willing to admit.

"Paxton," she said.

"He was the half-brother to your grandmother Inscho."

"Then what about—?" Blanch thought of the jumble of costumes, and fragments of speeches and scenes, and awful deeds. But why go into them with Edna? After all, Blanch had the key. And she was a Stowe, or Paxton, or whatever—people of notoriously little talk. Yet she couldn't help marveling, "Then everybody was related, blood relations!"

"Yes. Your mother and our Benjamin had the same great-grandfather."

Milan seemed to be both boiling and trying to remain tactful. "I thought the geneticists killed a lot of those fears about cousins marrying. Studies of the Hutterites, for instance—"

"But it was the belief that was so destructive," Edna explained. "At that time people were terrified of such blood lines. And suspicions must have been rife in the family."

"And I think I've met every one of them!" Blanch said.

Edna's eyes flashed disapproval, then resignation, at the concept.

It was all so clear now, sorted out.

"Mrs. Pierson," Blanch said, "had daddy's jaw, I saw her. Strong as Paxton's, but shorter. Her daughter, who became Mrs. Inscho, was regal, gorgeous. She was a lady and idealistic. But spoiled as a child, and terribly sorry for herself when things went wrong. But overprotected. Both terrorized and spoiled by Paxton. I can imagine why. Blanch Locke was a pale shadow, a running down—"

"No," said Edna. "I think your grandmother knew more than the others—except Mrs. Pierson, of course—and it appalled her. By that time the biblical 'rods' of vengeance were less terrifying. But suddenly the whole mare's nest of psychoanalysis had come to offer even more frightening punishments. She was horrified at the possibility that your mother and Benjamin—"

"Then how could she have let them?" Blanch wailed.

"Because it was all hints, vague allusions. And

you can understand how especially frightened she must have been of implanting these fears if they were untrue."

"Then how do you know so much?" said Blanch.

"Aaron's discovery of documents. And because you seem to have proved everything."

"I?"

"I think I know what's been troubling you, and I'm afraid I can't help you. If you need any help," Edna added. She shook her head sadly from side to side, then smiled with tender sadness and said, "You're the horseshoe in the scientist's office for me. When he was chided about it, he said, 'I gather it works whether I believe it or not.' —And I don't know what to think."

"Then how do we know," Milan protested, "that any of these things you hint that Blanch— and incidentally, I too—encountered, ever actually happened? Maybe they were merely 'ideal' things, in the sense of ideas, desires, hates, mad dreams?"

"That is what's so sad," said Edna. "They may have been. But whether they had occurred or not, in whole or in part, all this unhappiness came about over little more than a sordid tribal tabu."

"But where does—what I *think* recently happened—leave me?" said Blanch, worried.

"I understand your distress," said Edna, her voice almost breaking. "It's a terrible thing when a child doesn't know it's own background. And I think Aaron and I were pushed into silence by first our suspicion—yes, we suspected too!—and then knowledge of all this sadness and madness of so many of your forebears. How Aaron suffered!"

"My mother too?"

Edna's eyes warmed. "She was wonderful. Liberal, affectionate. Oh, frivolous and queenlike too, but you just had to like her. Both she and Benjamin were uncontaminated."

Milan seemed troubled, hardly listened.

"Was there something," he said, "about a pony or colt murdered—"

The scar on Paxton's forehead! Could it have been—?

"And some powerful male dressed like a woman, or a woman more male than female—?"

Milan stopped. Edna had turned ashen.

"There are things that no matter how liberal I may seem to be, I find too base to consider," she said.

So that was something they would never know.

"And now," Edna said more gently, "if you'll leave me. I believe you brought the car. If you would leave that for me."

"Of course," said Milan.

Blanch went to Edna, was relieved and thankful to again sense the wall of diffidence recreating itself between them, a familiar and almost pleasant thing after what had been said. Not that it was all roses. Again Edna had that sad and curious look. Blanch interpreted it as reading: What will this knowledge do to you? Perhaps to Milan? Not, I hope, that you will regard it—nor disregard it.

Knowledge of what? Blanch wondered. False guilt—or hallucinations? Ancient blood curse—

or brain damage? There was always that to consider. And Edna, the great exponent of emotional
laissez-faire for everyman, was being true to herself by somehow communicating an awareness
of what little there was to do, in any case.

Blanch smiled, leaned over and kissed Edna's
yellow brow. She nodded to Milan. The two left.
Left an empty house.

The crystal star? Perhaps she would pick it up
later.

"I guess that takes care of everything," Milan
said quietly.

Blanch smiled, a tired, indifferent smile.

"I hope it does!" Milan said.

Was it possible that her operation somehow
tuned her in to those things that may have happened, or tuned them out of wherever they were
in limbo, wherever that was?

And where had Mr. Mallkin gone? Blanch wondered.

And what was happening to the big house? How
flat, suddenly, were the memories of the recent awful past, or all the memories Blanch cared to consider or had not buried through the censor in her
brain.

As they reached the highway Blanch turned.
The big house was indeed gone. Even by trying to
create within herself an empathy for it, she could
not see it.

They had started for Edna's house, but found
themselves walking beyond it.

"This is the end," Milan said to Blanch. "I

mean, I think we've got its number. We pushed
the red button on it. Do you think so?"

I hope so, Blanch thought, said nothing, smiled.
I hope so.

"I mean," Milan said, worried, "how many
mixed-up relatives can we have?"

Suddenly, realizing what he had said, he burst
into wild laughter, hugged her violently. It was
then Blanch felt that it might be all right.

GOTHIC MYSTERIES
*of Romance
and Suspense . . .*

by Rae Foley

DARK INTENT
FATAL LADY
GIRL ON A HIGH WIRE
THE HUNDREDTH DOOR
MALICE DOMESTIC
THE MAN IN THE SHADOW
NIGHTMARE HOUSE
NO HIDING PLACE
OMINOUS STAR
SLEEP WITHOUT MORNING
THE SHELTON CONSPIRACY
THIS WOMAN WANTED
WHERE IS MARY BOSTWICK?
WILD NIGHT

and Velda Johnston

ALONG A DARK PATH
THE FACE IN THE SHADOWS
HOUSE ABOVE HOLLYWOOD
THE MOURNING TREES
THE LIGHT IN THE SWAMP
THE PEOPLE ON THE HILL

Dell Books 75¢

If you cannot obtain copies of these titles from your local bookseller, just send the price (plus 15c per copy for handling and postage) to Dell Books, Post Office Box 1000, Pinebrook, N. J. 07058.

and Mary Roberts Rinehart

ALIBI FOR ISABEL
THE ALBUM
THE BAT
THE BREAKING POINT
THE CIRCULAR STAIRCASE
DANGEROUS DAYS
THE DOOR
THE FRIGHTENED WIFE
THE GREAT MISTAKE
HAUNTED LADY
LOST ECSTASY
THE MAN IN LOWER TEN
THE RED LAMP
THE STATE VS ELINOR NORTON
THIS STRANGE ADVENTURE
THE STREET OF SEVEN STARS
THE WINDOW AT THE WHITE CAT

Dell Books 75¢

If you cannot obtain copies of these titles from your local bookseller, just send the price (plus 15c per copy for handling and postage) to Dell Books, Post Office Box 1000, Pinebrook, N. J. 07058.

HOW MANY OF THESE DELL BESTSELLERS HAVE YOU READ?

If you cannot obtain copies of these titles from your local bookseller, just send the price (plus 15c per copy for handling and postage) to Dell Books, Post Office Box 1000, Pinebrook, N. J. 07058.